Other books by H. Allen Smith

THE
GREAT
CHILI
CONFRONTATION

A DRAMATIC HISTORY OF
THE DECADE'S MOST IMPASSIONED
CULINARY EMBROILMENT
(WITH RECIPES)

BY

H. Allen Smith

TRIDENT PRESS · NEW YORK

ACKNOWLEDGMENTS

THE GREAT CHILI CONFRONTATION originally appeared in a condensed version in Holiday
Magazine, ©, 1968, by the Curtis Publishing Company.

Chapter 2 originally appeared in a slightly altered
version in Holiday Magazine, ©, 1967, by H. Allen
Smith.

Chapter 9 ("Green Bottles Down the Rio Grande")
is reprinted courtesy of Field & Stream.

SBN: 671–27023–0

Library of Congress Catalog Card Number: 69–13008

To Wick Fowler

WARNING!
Speed-reading is strictly forbidden in this book.

THE
GREAT
CHILI
CONFRONTATION

ONE

At precisely 11:43 of the clock on a fair October morning in 1967 two male humanoids stood on the veranda of a crumbling adobe building in the ghost town of Terlingua, Texas, and listened to the thump of a wooden spoon against an ancient copper washboiler.

The dull thump signaled the start of an event that all but eliminated international tensions and domestic tribulations from the front pages of Texas newspapers. It was the bitterly fought contest called The Great Chili Confrontation and its story shall dwell forever in the pages of history. Forever, in Texas, is approximately a year and a half.

The two combatants, each claiming to be the world's champion cooker of chili con carne, were of inharmonious physical dimensions. One was a citizen of Austin denominated Wickford P. Fowler, a man who would butcher at better than 250 pounds. He stood behind his pot as *agent provocateur* of the Chili Appreciation Society International, a local group in Dallas. All things in Dallas are International, save only those that are Outer Spatial.

The second man was a trim, vibrant-looking, insouciant, velvet-voiced dashing fellow—a slightly graying Lochinvar who had come out of the East and who was now wearing the colors of the Fighting Bucks of Alpine, Texas. A fighting buck of Alpine, Texas, is a high school football player. This second man, this magnetic person, was the author of the history you are reading. I have reference to me.

That these two men should stand on this veranda with large spoons in their hands, Jim Bowie, Davey Crockett, and Claude Fetridge gave up their lives in the Alamo at San Antonio de Bexar.

Spread out in front of the Terlingua Inn, where the Chili War reached its dreadful culmination, were upward of a thousand spectators representing all walks of human life plus some as yet unwalked. A few miles up the dusty road, called the Wetback Expressway, at the Terlingua airstrip ordinarily used by the Border Patrol, stood twenty-odd planes that had brought people in from New York, Los Angeles, Dallas, Austin, San Antonio, and the nearby megalopolis of Alpine, eighty miles straight north.

On the veranda where the chili was soon bubbling a jazz band from Fort Stockton played a steady accompaniment. Cameras and crews from four television stations were present. Every second man, it seemed, toted a radio mike and tape recorder, and there was no counting the still cameras that were in action. The *Wall Street Journal* and *Sports Illustrated* and the London *Daily Mirror* and *Texas Parade* were represented. The AP and UPI had their Number One Texas correspondents on the scene. Also present was a gentleman named Ormly Gumfudgin who said he represented the *Wretched Mess News* of West Yellowstone, Montana.

Planes flashed back and forth across the brassy sky and some of these scattered leaflets propagandizing the crowd on behalf of Texas industry, Texas womanhood, and Texas period. Six young women described as Swedish movie actresses (and looking it) had been flown in from Hollywood, along with six spectacular flower-power hippies.

A grizzled rancher from over toward Presidio was heard to

say: "Never seen such a mangy crowd in the Big Bend country since Pancho Villa was raidin' acrost the Rio Grande."

Someone else remarked that the Tex–Mex border had not witnessed such colorful doin's since the Fitzsimmons–Maher heavyweight championship fight was staged by Judge Roy Bean on a sandbar just below the town of Langtry.

How did all this come about? Who erred? Why this antic madness in Terlingua? It is a small place, its population estimated at between none and five. It is a city so distant from civilized climes that some say it costs 48 cents to mail a nickel postcard to it or from it. An improbable backdrop for such a mighty happening.

Sufficient time has now passed for tempers to have cooled, for ragged nerves to have relaxed. I undertake this formalized and definitive history of The Confrontation after a period of earnest soul-searching, and because the Durants have thrown in the sponge. I have reference to Will and Ariel Durant who, after many years of backbreaking toil on their great Story of Civilization series of histories, have quit. Their tenth and final volume has brought them down to the storming of the Bastille, an event of minor importance when viewed alongside the Chili Wrangle. And so the Durants will never achieve the point in history where they might consider the square-off at Terlingua. It is unfortunate that they cannot continue their work right down to the Chili War. But there is satisfaction and solace in the fact that I am here to take over. Scholars among my readers (in case any should get hold of this book) will be quick to recognize that I have followed the Durant pattern in organizing this history. And a bit later I shall state my qualifications as a foodstuff historian.

The Great Chili Confrontation had its true genesis in mid-afternoon of a gray December day in the year preceding Terlingua. On that day I went into the kitchen of my home thirty-five miles north of Rockefeller Center and placed a heavy iron pot on the stove. It was my birthday and, such being the condition of my life at the time, the wildest thing I could think of to do by way of celebration was to make a pot of chili.

There was nothing at all special or remarkable about this procedure. I have been making pots of chili as long as I can remember. In fact I am able to demonstrate that I go back a long way as a chili-maker. Nigh onto thirty years ago I published a book called *Low Man on a Totem Pole* in which, among other things, I recounted a few adventures I had as a young newspaperman in Denver. I wrote of a certain professor of Greek who quit teaching at Harvard and wound up as a reporter on the Denver *Post,* where I was employed. This man, this professor, was eccentric. He was so thoroughly eccentric that we, the wild ones of the Denver *Post* staff, enjoyed his company and invited him into our councils. In that early book, then, will be found these paragraphs:

> One evening I threw a chili party at my home and invited this same ex-professor. He spent the entire evening waltzing with a straight-back chair which he called Xanthippe. Whenever the phonograph stopped he'd go to it and feed it chili.
>
> "The little thing needs sustenance," he would say. He jammed it full of chili, and it was never of any use after that. And when the evening was over I took him to the door. He was a dignified man and there was dignity in the arch of his neck as he glanced back into the room for a final affectionate look at Xanthippe. In parting he said:
>
> "I want you to know that I have had the finest time of my life tonight. And I want to compliment you on your chili. It was better than Childs'."

Now that I copy those lines I suspect I may be making a mistake by reprinting them here. The compliment the professor paid my chili was not precisely unequivocal. Someone among my enemies might very well say that the professor was actually putting the knock on my chili; someone among my enemies might even contend that my chili was so miserable that it would gag a victrola. Yet I'm going to let the passage stand as proof of the fact that I am no newcomer to the ranks of chili-heads. I have had long experience with it.

On my birthday, then, I got the meat seared and put in some tomato paste and added some water and got the various flavorings ready. I remember that particular pot of chili quite well for two reasons. First, because it was that birthday batch that really led to The Trouble and, second, accidentally I hit the handle of the big spoon with my elbow, springboarding it out of the pot and showering red goo all over the stove and all over my pantaloons. I spoke a four-letter word which ranks as an important and significant expression in American folk-say, employed nowadays by both men and women; I spoke it on my birthday and I freely admit that my own personal everyday speech would be seriously crippled if I were forbidden the use of that word in moments of chagrin and disgust. Having uttered it loud and clear, I went along with the job of cooking the chili. It is good for the soul, sometimes, to speak in terms of basic scatology.

Into that birthday pot I put some sweet basil which I grew myself, and the quintessential cumin seed* and a bit of salt and oregano and chili powder and Ac'cent. It was time now for a long period of gentle simmering—at least two hours. I turned the fire low and went to my study to work on a magazine article entitled *Duck Calls in the Dining Car.* I

---

* Elliott Arnold, the novelist, once cross-examined me on the subject of chili manufacture. I recited off the list of ingredients and when I came to cumin seed he stopped me. "Hold it, pal," he protested. "Let's keep the record straight. Don't try to tell *me* that there's something called cumin seed. I can take so much, and no more." I went out and bought him a jar.

make haste to say that I did not put any shredded bell pepper into the pot. Someone else would take care of that, on the sly. Details of this underhanded interference will be spread on the record in due time.

Along about 6 o'clock that December evening I went back to the kitchen and tasted the chili. It was superb. Just right. Possibly the best batch I had ever put together. I tasted it again, savoring the high flavor and the bite of it, and then I said, speaking to nobody, "It is an infernal bleeding god damned shame that the rest of the world should be deprived of this noble ambrosia. I think I ought to do something about it." I love my fellowman. At times.

The next day I finished *Duck Calls in the Dining Car*, whirled a fresh sheet of paper into my typewriter, and started immediately on an article about my chili.

At that moment in history the world was moving along its traditional course . . . the course of balanced wisdom, of brotherhood, of universal integrity. Events were proceeding on an even keel. People were behaving as they have always behaved. Pippa passed, singing her song. There was no way for me to know that my birthday pot of chili would, in the end, shake the very underpinnings of the earth; there was no way for me to know that insidious forces were abroad in the land, waiting to slug me in the chops. I had no inkling that events would develop, ominous events, the way the Civil War grew out of small beginnings—Dred Scott going about his business of digging taters, Abe Lincoln mooning around in his shawl, Old Ed Stanton casually whipping the bejezus out of his slaves out there in Steubenville, Jeff Davis ginning his cotton and downing his juleps, and the gentle Marse Robert E. Lee off yonder teaching 'rithmetic or whatever the hell it was he was doing. It was that way. No hint of the great crashing events to come, of passions that would be inflamed —so much so that relations between the United States and the Arab nations would be brought to the breaking point.

No. Wait. That's not right. That was a *theory* only, postu-
lated by a pleasant lady who stood for a while at my elbow
while I was cooking at Terlingua.

Out of the swelling goodness of my heart I had set forth to
tell the American public something of the joy to be had from
good chili, properly confected, and from this benevolent and
altruistic act would spring a harvest of evil—a series of
vituperative attacks against me, calumniations, jeremiads,
defamations, and vilifications the like of which had not been
witnessed since Senator Joe McCarthy left the scene.

The time of the culmination at Terlingua . . . well, it is a
shame that Thomas Wolfe is no longer alive; he could
furnish an adequate prose style descriptive of the state of
the nation at the moment of The Great Confrontation. At
least he could work in a lot of place names and Arapahoe crap
and railroad stations and all that. Ah, well, we can't have
everything.

The article which I began composing the day after my
birthday and which I finished about a week later appeared
the following August in *Holiday* Magazine under the title,
Nobody Knows More About Chili Than I Do. A *casus belli*,
instanter. In the overall picture it became known as The
Pragmatic Sanction. It set the jackals of Texas and particularly the hungry hyenas of Dallas against me, in full cry. It
drove grown but immature men to commit excesses un-
matched since the Borgias strode the Roman turf. I reprint
it now substantially the way it was published. . . .

TWO

THE PRAGMATIC SANCTION:

When I was a boy of ten in Decatur, Illinois, my mother gave me twenty cents every morning—half of it for carfare to school, the remaining dime for my lunch. I could have spent that dime on candy or ice cream, but I can't recall that I ever did, because it was at this magic and benign moment in time that I discovered chili.

Day after day I went to Chili Bill's joint a couple of blocks from the school, sat at a scrubbed wooden counter, and for my ten cents got a bowl of steaming chili, six soda crackers, and a glass of milk. That was livin'!

I have been a chili man ever since those days. Nay, I have been *the* chili man. Without chili I believe I would wither and die. I stand without a peer as a maker of chili, and as a judge of chili made by other people. No living man, and let us not even think of women in this connection, *no living man,* I repeat, can put together a pot of chili as ambrosial, as delicately and zestfully flavorful, as the chili I make. This is a fact so stern, so granitic, that it belongs in the encyclopedias, as well as in all standard histories of civilization.

That is the way of us chili men. Each of us knows that *his* chili is light-years beyond other chili in quality and singularity; each of us knows that all other chili is such vile slop that a coyote would turn his back on it.

My brother Sam believes that he should be given the Nobel prize for chili-making. He and I didn't speak for a year and a half because of our clash of views on chili-making. Word got to me that Sam was telling people that our Pop had called him the greatest chili-maker in all Christendom. I knew this to be a falsehood; my father had said that *I* was the greatest. My sister Lou tried to de-escalate our feud by saying that Pop actually had remarked that *he* was the greatest chili-maker in the civilized world.

Brother Sam has gone along for years making chili without so much as a whiff of cumin seed in it, and cumin seed is as essential to chili as meat is to a hamburger. I was at Sam's house once and in a moment of fraternal feeling ate a spoonful of his foul chili. I remarked helpfully that it had no cumin seed in it, and Sam said that I could leave his fireside and never come back. "One bowl of your chili," said I, "would pollute the waters of the Great Salt Lake." And off I stomped.

Thus began the feud, and it came to an end only after news reached me that Sam was warring on another chili front. He and I both believe that proper chili should be soupy, with lots of broth. He has a friend named VanPelt who composes thickened chili, Texas-style. My chili and Sam's chili are eaten with a soup spoon; VanPelt eats his from a plate with a fork. Sam and VanPelt broke off relations for a while after a highly seasoned argument over thin-versus-thick. VanPelt contended that Sam's chili should be eaten through a straw, and Sam said that VanPelt's lavalike chili could be molded into balls and used to hold down tent flaps in a high wind. I was proud of my brother after that; he stood firm against the wretched sort of chili that is eaten from a plate with a fork.

There are fiends incarnate, mostly Texans, who put

chopped celery in their chili, and the Dallas journalist Frank X. Tolbert, who has been touted as the Glorious State's leading authority on chili, throws in cornmeal. Heaven help us one and all! You might as well throw in some puffed rice, or a handful of shredded alfalfa, or a few Maraschino cherries. There's an old Texas saying that would seem to apply here. It originated in the cow camps and concerned any range cook whose grub was consistently miserable. Of him the cowhands would grumble, "He ain't fit to tote guts to a bear." That, precisely, is what I say of Mr. Frank X. Tolbert.

You may suspect, by now, that the chief ingredients of all chili are fiery envy, scalding jealousy, scorching contempt, and sizzling scorn. The quarreling that has gone on for generations over New England clam chowder versus Manhattan clam chowder (the Maine Legislature once passed a bill outlawing the mixing of tomatoes with clams) is but a minor spat alongside the raging feuds that have arisen out of chili recipes.

A fact so positive as the fact that chili was invented by Texans will, by the very nature of its adamantine unshakability, get shook. Lately it has become fashionable to say that chili—contrary to all popular belief—was first devised by Mexicans and then appropriated by the Texans. Some of the newer cook books come right out and say that chili is the national dish of Mexico. In Elena Zelayeta's *Secrets of Mexican Cooking* it is asserted that the popular Mexican dish, *Carne en Salsa de Chile Colorado*—meat in red chili sauce —is much the same as the chili con carne of Texas. "It is a famous Mexican dish," says Senora Zelayeta, "that has been taken and made famous by the Lone Star State." This lady, one of the most respected of contemporary authorities on Mexican cuisine, then proceeds to destroy every shred of her authority by suggesting that a can of hominy goes well in a pot of chili.

On the other hand, if there is any doubt about what the

generality of Mexicans think about chili, the *Diccionario de Mejicanismos*, published in 1959, defines chili con carne as "detestable food passing itself off as Mexican, sold in the U.S. from Texas to New York." The Mexicans in turn get told off in a 14th-century *Herball, or General Historie of Plantes*, in which is written of the chile pepper: "It killeth dogs."

I am a frequent visitor in Mexico, and once, in a sportive mood, I decided to introduce chili into Mexico, get the Mexicans to making it in their homes, and setting up chili joints along the highways. I have a good friend, once a novice bullfighter who failed at that trade, who is maître d'hôtel of a large restaurant. When he found out what I was doing, he spoke to me in soft and liquid accents: "If I ever hear you spick the word of chili con carne one more time in our beloved raypooblica, *pues,* I am not in the custom of spitting in the eye of gringos, but I will spit in your eye with glory and speed and hardness." He didn't make it with the bulls but I felt that he could make it with me, and so I gave up the chili-con-carnization of Mexico. °

One present-day dabbler in chili lore has come up with a shocking discovery which he believes is proof that chili con carne had its origin in Mexico. Cited is the classic work by Bernal Diaz del Castillo, which chronicles the invasion of Mexico City by Cortez and his conquistadores in the 16th century. Diaz reports that he witnessed a ceremony in which some of his Spanish compadres were sacrificed by Aztec priests, and then butchered; chunks of conquistadore meat were thrown to the populace, and these people rushed home and cooked them with hot peppers, wild tomatoes, and an herb that apparently was oregano. That, my friends, is seriously set down as the true origin of chili. I dislike having

° I was a bit disturbed that the ex-bullfighter took me seriously, fearing that I might be Thirty-threed out of the country—a brisk Mexican legal procedure in which an offensive foreigner is thrown so far out of the raypooblica that he hits Saskatchewan on the first bounce.

21

to say it, but if you are going to adopt this recipe, it must begin, "First, catch yourself a lean Spaniard. . . ."

I know of only one Texan who has the facts straight on the origin of chili—Charles Ramsdell, author of an excellent history of San Antonio. It is clear from his delvings, as well as my own, that chili con carne had its beginnings in San Antonio. Was it a dish contrived by Mexicans of old San Antonio de Bexar? No. Was it put together by white Texans? Not at all. You'd never guess in eight centuries. Chili was invented by Canary Islanders. In the 1720's the Spanish were in command of the town, which they had founded, but the French were pushing in from the east, and an appeal went out to the King of Spain to send some settlers. The King obliged halfheartedly, shipping sixteen families out from the Canary Islands. They established themselves in rude huts on the spot now know as the Main Plaza. In their homeland, these people were accustomed to food made pungent with spices. They liked hot peppers and lots of garlic and they were acquainted with oregano. So they looked around to see what was available in foodstuffs in their new home, and they came up with a stew of beef and hot peppers and oregano and garlic and, I make bold to believe, tomatoes and onions and beans. It is my guess, too, that they managed to get hold of some cumin seed, which comes chiefly from North Africa. That's the way it happened, and any Texas historians who dispute me can go soak their heads.

Let it be understood that I am well disposed toward Texans and enjoy visiting their State; I'm tolerant of all their idiotic posturing, of every one of their failings, save only this arrant claim of superiority in the composing of chili. Mr. Tolbert, of Dallas, who appears to be spokesman for the Chili Appreciation Society International, declares that acceptable chili should contain no tomatoes, no onions, and no beans. This is a thing that passeth all understanding, going full speed. It offends my sensibilities and violates my mind.

Mr. Tolbert even criticizes Lyndon Johnson's chili recipe because it leaves out beef suet and includes tomatoes and onions. Yet the LBJ chili contains no beans. To create chili without beans, either added to the pot or served on the side, is to flout one of the basic laws of nature. I've been told that when I was a baby and it came time to wean me, I was fed Eagle Brand milk with navy beans frappéed into it. Thereafter, all through childhood and adolescence, I ate beans three or four times a week. If Chili Bill, back there in Illinois, had served his chili without beans, I would surely have deserted him and bought chocolate sodas for my lunch.

Texas has at least one chili scholar owning a glimmer of intelligence: Maury Maverick, Jr., son of the former Mayor of San Antonio and Rooseveltian Congressman. The younger Maury is a lawyer, and a true chili man in one respect—he speaks out against other chili cooks, saying, for example, of California chili: "With all that god damn sweet stuff in it, it's like eating a strawberry sundae."

As for Southern California, my friend Fred Beck, a gourmet and semiprofessional wine taster, adduces evidence to suggest that Los Angeles is the chili capital of the world. (That title, by the way, is claimed by San Antonio, by Springfield, Illinois, and by the tiny ghost town of Terlingua in the Big Bend country, and lately by Dallas.)

Mr. Beck tells me that chili was once called "size" in the town known to him as Lil-ole-ell-ay. "Size" came into usage by way of one Ptomaine Tommy, once proprietor of the largest and best-known chili parlor in the city. Ptomaine Tommy served straight chili and an epical southwestern variation, a hamburger smothered with chili. He had two ladles, a large and a small. When a customer ordered straight chili, he got the large ladle. When he wanted the other, he usually said, "Hamburger size." So Ptomaine Tommy put up one sign that said Hamburger Size 15¢ and another that said Chili Size 20¢. Other chili joints followed suit, and before long chili was known throughout Los Angeles as "size." They'd say, "Just gimme a bowl of size."

Mr. Beck speaks, too, of the era when the architecture went kooky in Los Angeles, and commercial structures were designed to suggest the nature of the trade conducted within. There was a building on Pico shaped like a coffeepot, with steam issuing from its spout. A weenie stand on La Cienega was a large and hideous representation of a frankfurter. Then came the chain of Chili Bowls. It was quickly noted by the always perceptive Angelenos that these structures were shaped like giant chamberpots, sans handles, so it became customary to say, "Let's drive over to the pisspot for a bowl of chili."

During my probings into the story of chili I stumbled upon a fact that made my heart leap. There is a town called Chili in my State, New York. Texans pay not even lip service to their chili, for they have no town of that name. As for the New York community, just west of Rochester (there is also a North Chili nearby), I was soon disillusioned.

I telephoned my friend Judge Ray Fowler of Rochester. "Why," I asked him, "did they call the town of Chili by that name?"

"Never heard of it," said Judge Fowler. "How do you spell it?"

I spelled it.

"Oh," he exclaimed, "you mean Chy-lye. The early settlers named it in honor of Chile's breaking away from Spanish rule."

"So," I said, "they misspelled it, and then mispronounced it. And it has nothing to do with chy-lye con carne?"

"Nothing at all."

Just writing about this matter makes me disconsolate, so let us pass on to the chy-lye that comes in a bowl. The secret of making superior chili lies first in the ingredients and second in the genius of the cook. Nothing should ever be measured. Experimentation is the thing. Those blessed Canary Islanders in San Antonio wouldn't have known a measuring spoon from an electric carving knife. Spanish cook books never issue peremptory orders, for that would not be polite. They speak of "maybe fifteen centavos worth" of parsley, a half a handful of so-and-so, and maybe a bunch of butter, and a few "teeth" of garlic if you have some in the house.

My daughter follows my haphazard methods and turns out chili that is the sensation of her set. She says she passes my recipe along to her chili-loving friends, and converts the ignorant to it, and all hands proclaim it to be the best of all possible chilis. That's what she tells me. Whenever I hear those heartwarming reports I feel so bucked up that I give her a trip to Mexico or Puerto Rico. Much the same thing happens in the case of my son, though he tells me he composes my chili with the doors locked and the shades drawn. He lives in Texas. For a time I wanted to establish that lovely tradition, the old family recipe, a secret that wild horses couldn't drag out of my descendants. A family is not a true entity unless it has in its archives a fabulous secret recipe. But my formula is out, and rapidly spreading, so I give it to the world. . . .

(At this point in The Pragmatic Sanction, as it was published in *Holiday*, I make my move as they say at the horse tracks. Please note the emphasis I have placed on the fact that I never really make chili the same way twice—that it's a matter of continuing experimentation, tasting, then tasting again, until it comes just right. So now I undertake a few subtle changes in my recipe. In the months since The Pragmatic Sanction was published I have had much advice from the outside world, and I have experimented, and I think I've made a few improvements on my formula. The recipe that

25

follows is not precisely the same as the published one, though it is close. I make haste to say that none of the improvements came from a Texan.)

CHILI H. ALLEN SMITH

Make sure you have good meat—three pounds of lean chuck, or round, or tenderloin tips. Be sure the meat is trimmed down to where there is not a shred of gristle in it. Texans are great gristle-eaters and I find most of their chili inferior for that and other reasons. The poor creatures just don't know any better. Out, then, with all gristle! Have the meat coarse-ground. Sear it in an iron kettle. If you don't have an iron kettle you are not civilized; go out and get one. Don't break up the chunks of beef. It is good to have lumpy meat in your chili. When you've got it seared, add one or two small cans of tomato paste or tomato sauce or if you want to use fresh or canned tomatoes put them through a colander. Now chop one or two onions and, if you hanker for it, half a bell pepper. Add these ingredients to the pot with about a quart of water. Crush a couple or more cloves of garlic and then add about half a teaspoon of oregano, maybe a couple of pinches of sweet basil, and a quarter teaspoon of cumin seed or cumin powder. A lady in San Diego has written me that she buys the cumin seed whole, roasts it in an iron skillet, then uses a rolling pin to convert it into a powder—she says store-bought cumin powder can become stale. A perfectionist. Now put in some salt and for a starter, two tablespoons of chili powder. If you can get the Chimayo ground chiles, packaged in Albuquerque, do so by all means. I will speak of it later, for I think it is the best I've ever used. Sometimes when they are available I use chile pods but don't be skittish about using a good brand of chili powder. Simmer your chili for an hour and a half or longer, adding some Ac'cent to sharpen the flavor, and then about ten minutes from conclusion, add your beans.

Use pinto beans if you can get them; if they are not available, canned kidney beans will do. Simmer a bit longer, doing some tasting and, as the *Gourmet Cookbook* has it, "correct seasoning." When you've got it right, to suit your personal taste, let it set a while. It will taste better the second day, still better the third, and absolutely superb the fourth. Texans consider it a bloody sacrilege to cook beans with their chili. I say they're all daft. They also scream bloody murder at the idea of any sweet pepper being included. You'll have to make up your own mind—just don't let their raucous way of talking overpower you. One final personal note: I cannot eat chili without a large glass of cold milk at my elbow. No beer, no water, no wine —just cold milk.

I deem it a pleasure to have given you my recipe for chili. I can only say in conclusion that some people are born to the tragic life. There are three distressing physiological mistakes made by nature: the vermiform appendix, the prostate gland, and the utter inability of many people to eat chili because of delicate digestive tracts.

I really bleed for them.

The End

Thus The Pragmatic Sanction. I think the thesis is clear, the writing is pellucid, the prose is limpid, there can be no mistake about the *leitmotiv*—the principal argument. The mood is sustained and adequately subjunctive. Let us be conservative and say that what we have here is a prose poem. And the argument is: every man who cooks chili believes with all his heart that his chili is infinitely superior to all other chili on earth.

That one man should arise and challenge this thesis would seem to be ridiculous; yet a phalanx of two hundred and nine men in Dallas, Texas, arose and cried out in a fury: "Fiddle-faddle! Sassy-frass!"

It is needful that I explain why I singled out the chili-heads of Texas for criticism; I did so because they are the *loudest* of all chili-heads on this earth. My attitude toward them was not predicated on hearsay. I had been spending some time in Texas, doing research on a novel I was writing, a novel about a multimillionaire cat. And now, having finished the chili essay for *Holiday*, I went back to Texas, into the very jaws of Hell—to Galveston and then Corpus Christi and Alpine and finally to a little Rio Grande mining village called La Linda.

Before I proceed with an account of fresh adventures in the Lone Star State, let me caution you once again—don't cook your chili by rule and by rote. Compose it to suit your personal taste and the taste of your family. That is the basic thing.

THREE

There will be occasional digressions in this book, as there
are in all competent historical works. Your skilled historian
must abandon his main theme from time to time and venture
into the sideroads. If he knows his business he becomes the
shunpiker of literature—his tangents often have tangents
springing from them; his fleas hath smaller fleas that on them
prey; and these have smaller still to bite 'em; and so proceed
ad infinitum.

I call the reader's attention to the historical works of
Washington Irving, and the semiclassical books of Hubert
Quotts; also the earlier works of Biltmore Tingley as well as
Virgil Muslim's studies of the French and Indian Wars.
Perhaps the most famous example of how the digression may
be used to great effect in the writing of history is that of
Castro Tinklepaugh. Professor Tinklepaugh, in his work on
General Custer, got off his main theme and onto another
topic and never made it back; today his book is considered
to be the definitive treatment of sticky and dry cerumen in
American Indians. Cerumen, or earwax, occurs in two
phenotypic forms—sticky (wet) and dry (hard), and the
quality of cerumen is controlled by a single pair of genes in
which the allele for the sticky trait is dominant over the dry,
and that's a fact. Professor Tinklepaugh was at Chapter

Twenty-Eight of his halfway monumental work on the life of Custer when he got involved with Indian earwax and, as noted, he never was able to struggle back to his mainstream. Custer was forgotten and the rest of the book was filled with such fascinating detail as:

> Table 1 summarizes the data on families for which parental matings of earwax types, sticky x sticky, sticky x dry, and dry x dry, were available for study. Despite the small number of families available, our findings indicate that the inheritance of earwax in American Indians is similar to that described by Matsunaga for the Japanese, in which the sticky allele is dominant over the dry. In no instance did a parental mating of dry x dry produce children having sticky cerumen.

One is happy for Professor Tinklepaugh's digression.

Parenthetically, let me remark that there is a Texas connection here. Professor Tinklepaugh spent his final years doing cerumen research in association with Professor Andrew D. Robinson at the Sam Houston Institute of Technology—a school which, incidentally, has been in the news recently. At the urgent request of its cheerleaders, the Sam Houston Institute of Technology changed its name to the Sam Houston Technological Institute. Created quite a furore.

With such noteworthy precedents to guide me, I have no hesitation in undertaking a digression at this point in our history. It begins with the arrival of Cobberleigh, the book publisher, at my house in Westchester County, New York. Cobberleigh came for a long weekend and even though my principal business is the writing of books, his was a social visit and I made my usual firm decision not to talk shop. I took Cobberleigh out and let him watch me do a little weed-scratching around my plum tomatoes and my five varieties of hot peppers, including those grown from seed brought to me by Desmond Slattery from the jungles of British Honduras. All the while I kept spinning off hilarious anecdotes about my years as a grower of vegetables. He didn't say much beyond "Hmmmmmmmmm."

In the living room I had a handsome instrument which the English call, with some contempt, an electrified organ, and so I fixed Cobberleigh a stiff drink and then played him a few tunes, remarking that I had taught myself to do this marvelous thing, without previous acquaintance with any other musical instrument and without the ability to read a note of music. Inadvertently I mentioned an idea I once had to write a book on the theory of music, *my* theory of music, with the highly marketable title, *To Hell With Middle C.* Cobberleigh just sat there, sipping his drink. Tone deaf, probably.

In the meantime I had planned out almost all of the weekend cooking. I worked up a batch of my spaghetti sauce—the sensation of the immediate neighborhood, and Cobberleigh said it was good. The next day I spent several hours preparing *huachinango veracruz,* a method of baking red snapper as practiced by the people of Veracruz in Mexico. The way I do it is out of this planet, in the opinion of certain of my warmest friends.

While eating the *huachinango* Cobberleigh said, quite distinctly, "Nice." I already had a pot of chili in the refrigerator and was simply biding my time. I wanted to work up to it gradually, before knocking him over.

I told him about my celebrated New York Times Beef Stew. It is called New York Times Beef Stew because some years back my recipe appeared in that splendid, well-edited newspaper. One morning a Miss Levin from the *Times* woman's page came upcountry to interview my wife on what it is like to be married to an author. Such an one as me. My wife was in a highly humorous and whimsical mood that day, and told Miss Levin that it is a fate somewhat worse than death to be married to an author, such an one as me. Her own author, she said, is underfoot from morning to night, snoops on her telephone conversations, and takes the lids off pots and sniffs at things and says needs bay leaf.

It came on lunchtime that day and I served my beef stew. Miss Levin took one taste and then, with Sulzbergerian restraint, said, "My this is nice soup." I responded pettishly that it wasn't soup, it was beef stew. I then told her all about it, and she wrote down the recipe, even though I explained carefully—as always—that I never make it the same way twice. "Takes all the adventure out of cooking," I said, "if you follow a blueprint." A few days later my beef stew appeared in the *Times* along with a few inconsequential and frivolous remarks by my wife.

So I told all this to Cobberleigh and he put the ends of his fingers together and closed his eyes briefly, simulating thought, and then he said, "How would you like to try a cook book for us?"

"Strange you should suggest such a thing," I said, "because a neighbor of mine, Carla Rogers, has been clamoring for me to do a cook book for years. Carla is a knowledgeable gal, a fine cook herself, went to three colleges, hates pop art, and says dichotomy quite a lot. She's a complete nut on Mexican cuisine, and that happens to be my specialty."

This is all quite true about Carla Rogers. She always has my best interests at heart and about once a month gives me a new idea for a book. Let me cite an example of how she tries to be helpful. A few years back I spent two weeks in the hospital and she telephoned to jolly me up and she said, "What on earth do you do with your time in that place?"

I replied, "Nothing. My day starts with a happy little alcohol rub for breakfast and from then on deteriorates. There's no place to go but the bathroom."

She went into modified hysterics, simply split her sides.

"You've *got* to write a book with that title!" she cried. "*No Place to Go but the Bathroom!* A perfect title for you!"

32

She kept at me doggedly for a long time, for she is a woman of perseverance. It became a passion with Carla— getting me to write a book under that title. Now and then she sent postcards containing nothing but the lettering: NO PLACE TO GO BUT THE BATHROOM.

Cobberleigh the publisher seemed impressed by the fact that a woman who says dichotomy quite a lot would feel that I ought to undertake a cook book. So I pressed on.

"I'll tell you this," I said, firming my voice and trying to sound gritty and authoritative, I don't intend to do *just another* cook book. I intend to think up a gimmick, some- thing that will capture public attention. Get them to talking."

"That's the ticket," said Cobberleigh. "Give it some thought and let me know."

Fired now with enthusiasm, I set up the new aluminum outdoor cooker and smoked a turkey, a job that requires basting the bird every fifteen minutes for five hours. Cobber- leigh ate some of it and said it was tasty and then went back to New York. Somehow I forgot all about the bait of chili in the refrigerator.

I spent several days searching for that gimmick. I soon noticed that other people had gone in for gimmicks—there was even a volume called *The Seducer's Cook Book,* which set me off on a train of philosophical speculation that was probably bad for my health.

Then Cobberleigh phoned. "I've been thinking," he said, "about that idea of mine to have you do a cook book for us. We don't want you to do *just another* cook book. What we need is a gimmick."

"You are *so* right!" I agreed. "I'll see what I can come up with."

"One gimmick," he said, "might be to write us a *funny* cook book. De-emphasize the actual cooking and bear down on the humorous anecdote."

I had heard of a volume called the *I Can't Cook Cookbook* and I thought that one was quite far out—about three light-years northeast of the Big Dipper, and I soon found out that I had a lot to learn in the gimmick department. Off I went to the bookstores and the public library just in time to witness the arrival of Corinne Griffith's "fabulous new cookbook" called *I Can't Boil Water.** Then I came across one titled *I Hate to Cook Book* and another called *I Never Cooked Before Cook Book*. It began to appear that a lot of people had beaten Cobberleigh to the gimmick of de-emphasizing cooking in their cook books.

In no time at all I was up to my apron strings in culinary literature, with and without gimmicks. I'm now convinced that there are more cook books in print today than there are books about the Civil War Between the States for Southern Independence. I listed twenty-eight different Chinese cook books, including works by Sou Chan, Dolly Chow, Grace Chew, Nancy Ma, and the Benedictine Sisters of Peking. I found eight books on how to cook in a chafing dish, including one titled *Wick and Lick*. (Great God in heaven!) There was a book of German sausage recipes called *Wurst You Were Here* and a Japanese snack book titled *Nippon These*. (Keee-ryst in the Andes!) I'm not making these things up; my principles wouldn't permit of such a thing.

There are in print a *Minneapolis Symphony Cookbook*, and books about cooking on boats, on cooking for the Army and the Air Force, how to cook wild game in Canada, cooking in a college residence hall (for women), how to cook for cowboys, *The Keep-Calm Cookbook*, *How to Plan Church Meals*, *Low Sodium Fat Controlled Cookbook*, *Eating in Bed Cook Book*, the *Can-Opener Cook Book* and *New Can-Opener Cook Book*, the *Too Hot to Cook Book* (you

---

* Wick Fowler of Austin, Texas, I learned later, has worked up a recipe for people who say they can't boil water. It begins this way: "First, take your water and marinate it in bourbon. . . ."

just set there and sweat), *Cook, My Darling Daughter,*
Pheasants for Peasants, Have Cook Will Marry, the *Bible*
Cookbook, Two Hundred Soups, a $5.95 volume called *The
Other Half of the Egg* containing 180 ways of using extra
yolks or whites, and a $10 book of recipes used by the cooks
in San Francisco fire houses.

The list goes on seemingly without end. There is *The
Working Wives' Cook Book,* described as "a blessing for the
busy wife who just doesn't have time to start fixing supper
after a hard day at the office." This must mean that the
husband does the cooking, but I didn't have much time for
confusion because my eye fell on another volume titled *1001
Ways to Please a Husband.* That one put me in a thoughtful
mood, but I shook it off quickly. There's an adventure-style
cook book called *Let's Eat at Home,* a bit too swashbuckling
for my blood, and two other gimmicks that made sense:
Simple Cooking for the Epicure and the *Instant Epicure
Cookbook.* One that perplexed me slightly was the *No Cooking Cookbook* which presumably tells you to go out in the
yard and chomp grass. There are books that instruct us
about cooking in Williamsburg, Virginia City, Greenwich,
on a southern plantation, in Alaska and Texas and Hawaii,
on Cape Cod, in caves, among the Pennsylvania Dutch, at
Key West, in Thomas Jefferson's house, on the eastern Shore
of Maryland, in chuck wagons, and at Christ Church in
Alexandria, Virginia. There are hefty books on cooking with
curry powder, honey, herbs, apples, homogenized hominy
grits, booze, oranges, mushrooms, nasturtiums, soybeans, beer,
and many other ingredients including, no doubt, assafiddity
(Illinois spelling) which would tend to sharpen up soups and
ward off rheumatism.

I had merely scratched the surface of available cook
books, and now *I* began to get a little light-headed in my
quest for a gimmick. Interesting titles began popping into
my head: *Lassie's Favorite Veal Dishes, 600 Ways to Serve*

Barium, Cooking for Kooks, Recipes for the Rejected, Cooking With Novocain, and *How to Prepare Rock Cornish Bald Eagle.*

There was one quote friend unquote to whom I broached my problem. It happens that he is a cynic, short on principles, lacking in good manners, altogether hateful and rotten. "You," he said, "are one of those insufferable amateur cooks who talk all the time about how you never follow any recipes. You never measure things. You say it takes all the adventure out of cooking if you follow a blueprint. Don't you realize that *every* amateur cook says exactly the same thing? It's getting to be a bore. So why don't you turn out a cook book with nothing in it but your miserable chili? Eight hundred different ways to make the same god damn lousy chili!"

This churl doesn't hold his liquor well.

For some reason I began getting depressed about it all. I thought of the time Jack Paar asked Dody Goodman why she had not, like everybody else in show business, written a book.

"They asked me to write a book," she said, "but all the subjects have been used up."*

I began to feel that I was facing the same dilemma. Cobberleigh wanted me to write a gimmicked cook book, but all the gimmicks had been used up.

Then Carla Rogers, my dilettante neighbor, telephoned and wanted to know if I had done anything about that book on my experiences in the hospital. I said I hadn't. She began acting real fretful and corrosive. I was on the verge of telling her about my cook book problem and then a horrible thought crossed my mind and I held my tongue.

I just *knew* she'd have had the solution for me. A great and happy blending of two ideas: *The No Place to Go but the Bathroom Cook Book.*

---

* Subsequently, as was inevitable, Dody Goodman wrote a book.

FOUR

Maury Maverick, Jr., of San Antonio, gave it the felicitous name: The Great Chili Confrontation. Mr. Maverick had been my friend in the past and, in fact, furnished me with some of the history of chili which I included in The Pragmatic Sanction in *Holiday*. He laid claim to an extensive knowledge of chili lore—he is a lawyer but he has a number of side interests, including an itch to write. And he is somewhat of a ladies' man so his interest was, in the main, concentrated around the celebrated Chili Queens of Old San Antone. He had a tendency to romanticize about them whereas I am fairly certain that they had faulty teeth and smelt bad. There were no Dolores del Rios amongst them. I have looked into their history a bit myself and I've found that they were named Rosa and Maria and Jovira and things like that. For a time the No. 1 Chili Queen was an Anglo blonde named Sadie. She put out for money.

During the period when I was first investigating chili in San Antonio I undertook a tour of the Gebhardt plant. In the area of canned chili I had always considered Gebhardt's product to be superior; I could have been wrong about this, for the reason that in the East some of the other processed brands were not well-known during the years when I stocked my shelves with canned chili against the time when

I wanted my chili in a hurry. Now that I know more about it, now that I have a closer acquaintanceship with Texas, I'm aware of the fact that some Texans lean toward other brands. In case you didn't know it the people of San Antonio are great consumers of Mexican fodder. They have some kind of a fiesta or parade every week. The King, or ruler, of one of the town's chief festivals used to be called Selamat. Tamales spelled backwards.

At this point I must note the entrance into chili history of a character out of medieval history—Westbrook Pegler. Back in 1951 Mr. Pegler was engaged in a spirited journalistic altercation with various Texas authorities on the relative merits of one chili recipe as against another, and Mr. Pegler spoke out strongly in favor of Gebhardt's as "the best put-up chili-con in the world." When this 1967 chili dispute got to going real good, Mr. Pegler spoke from the wilderness around Tucson. He excoriated eagles. He wrote a couple of letters to me, still contending for Gebhardt's, and then he launched a vitriolic assault on the eagles of Brewster County, Texas. He had had personal contact with those eagles and he told me to beware of them in the Big Bend country, that a Brewster County eagle was a worse bastard than Heywood Broun.

But let us get the chili picture down to date. Back in New York *Holiday* finally hit the stands with The Pragmatic Sanction and I was off enjoying myself in Texas, and in Brewster County where I ignored eagles. I was bothering my mind with matters unrelated to chili, never suspecting for a moment that a Tolbert Tantrum was in the offing. I think I was Cloralex fishin' in the Rio Grande when Frank X. Tolbert let go at me with his opening round of canister. Tolbert had recently produced a small book titled *A Bowl of Red* and this vest-pocket volume purported to be an accumulation of the sum total of human knowledge concerning chili. As is the way with wet-eared authors, unaccustomed to

38

the lores of the lit'ry life, Mr. Tolbert felt that by virtue of his pamphlet he stood forth as the final authority on chili and no other human being should deign to open his mouth on the subject. The final word had been writ. In his column headed "Tolbert's Texas" he cried "Havoc!" and let slip the dogs of chili. He referred to me as "operator of a Mount Kisco, N.Y., milking goat farm" and he accused me of borrowing freely from his puny book; he also charged me with flagrantly misquoting Charles Ramsdell, the San Antonio historian. Then he committed a criminal assault upon my chili. He wrote:

"Mr. Smith recites his personal chili recipe, which he calls the best in the universe. It's not really chili. It's a chili flavored beef-and-vegetable soup. And very, very soupy. Among the ingredients are tomato paste or canned tomatoes, or fresh tomatoes and bell peppers, and two or three medium-sized onions. He cooks pinto beans, or even kidney beans, right in with this mess, instead of cooking the pinto beans on the side as he should."

The Tolbert Tantrum was forwarded to me in Southwest Texas and my blood boiled. I got off a letter to Tolbert at once. Its text follows:

Mr. Tolbert:
    The only satisfaction I can get out of your vitriolic assault upon my good name lies in the fact that it appeared on the same page as an article purporting to show Jesus Christ was a professional cotton-picker riding a feisty and intractable mule. Some newspaper.
    I try to make allowance for the fact that your tripes have long since become pockmarked and withered from eating that mud-puddin' you Texans choose to call chili. I cannot hold still, however, for the imputation that I purloined material from your sleazy little chili book and from Charles Ramsdell's history of San Antonio. You fib. You prevaricate. You lie.

39

I wrote my *Holiday* article before I ever saw your book. If you were half as good a reporter as I am, you would have known that I told Margaret Cousins at Doubleday that I didn't want to see your misbegotten mishmash until I had completed my own essay. She wanted to send me the galley proofs but I told her to hold off, to wait until the bound copies were ready, by which time my article would be in the hands of my agent. I did not want to be corrupted with misinformation, I did not want to be influenced by slovenly writing, I did not want to be disoriented by a man already well-known for his chaotic sense of confusion worse confounded. In my article I mentioned the name of the churl Tolbert on the basis of a *Saturday Evening Post* article of his, and I mentioned it only to demonstrate the man's intrinsic foolishness and lack of taste.

Now, as for Ramsdell. Again you lie in your masa-fouled teeth. I said only that Ramsdell was correct in placing the origin of chili in San Antonio. When I wrote about the Canary Islanders, that was *me* talking, as any fourth-grader would have known at a glance. I got my information on the Canary Islanders and how they invented chili not from Ramsdell, but from the files of Maury Maverick, Jr., and from chili experts at the Gebhardt cannery in San Antonio. I went through the Gebhardt plant and questioned men who know chili, who *live* chili. I would never trust information obtained from a gathering of childish, semi-rumped Rotarian-type cracker-breakers in Dallas. It would not surprise me to learn that your Society opens its meetings by singing "I'm a Lit-tull Prairie Flower, I'm Growing Wilder Evv-ree Hour." And then breaking the crackers. The spectacle would lead Sam Houston to utter the devout wish that he'd never left Virginia.

Since your intemperate outburst of August 16th I have read through most of your book. For the record *you* "borrowed freely" from John Gerard, Dr. Albert F. Hill, Dr. Roy Nakayama, Ruth W. Sneed, Dr. Lora Shields, my old friend Jim Street, Harriet Spofford, O. Henry, George

Herter, Joe Cooper, Pepe Romero, Wick Fowler, an un-
named Mexican magazine . . . the list is too long, too tiring.
You copy so diligently from other people that I feel certain
the "X" in your name stands for Xerox. There is not a single
interesting fact or theory in your book that I would have borrowed except perhaps the Dave Chasen recipe for chili,
which is far closer to my own recipe than to anything you
Texans slosh together. Elizabeth Taylor has good taste. It
all adds up to this: you are burned and bugged because you
overlooked the basic, the salient fact that the Canary Islanders of Old San Antone originated chili.

My Kisco milking goats send a loud blat in your direction.

H. Allen Smith

Back at my home in New York a package and a letter
arrived from this Wick Fowler of Austin, Texas. The package contained an assortment of dangerous-looking powders
and philtres and stuff that looked like ground-up shagbark.
It appears that Mr. Fowler has a sort of chili factory in
Austin, packaging all the ingredients but the meat and
tomato sauce. This product is called "Wick Fowler's 2-Alarm
Chili" and the factory is known as the Caliente Chili Company.

"Word has reached me," said the letter from Mr. Fowler,
"that you have developed a recipe for the hottest chili in the
country, although the BTU rating was not recorded. Life in
a Chili Factory is much different than Life in a Putty Knife
Factory. . . . As chef for the Chili Appreciation Society
International, it is my duty to introduce real chili to Mount
Kisco. Under separate asbestos cover I am sending you four
packages of real chili ingredients . . . an item that is making nervous wrecks out of fire marshals. In Vietnam last year
I made a batch of chili which was spread over a jungle held
by the VC. The enemy thought it was a new napalm formula."

41

Subsequently I was able to address the following reply to Mr. Fowler, who was soon to become my arch-enemy in The Great Confrontation:

Mr. Wick Fowler,
P.O. Box 1444,
Austin, Tex., 78767.

Dear Mr. Fowler:

It crushes my very soul to have to do this, but I must tell you that you compose a very passable chili considering that you do it in Texas. It just damn near *kills* me to say that you construct a chili of superior quality. My toes curl within my shoes and smart like mad when I carry this praise a bit further and tell you that you make the best clod-whanged chili ever put together anywhere on earth outside of my own kitchen.

It must surely be that you have strong currents of northern blood coursing through your veins; it seems to me that, even though you might not know it yourself, when you were an infant you were kidnaped somewhere in the Middle West or East and spirited off to Texas, possibly by Kickapoo Indians or Canary Islanders. It is simply impossible that you could be an unsullied Texan, else you would not be able to carpenter up such a fine dish of chili as I had last evening and again today. For breakfast, by god! It is the first time I ever ate chili without beans *cooked in with the rest,* without beans at all. I found it a delight.

I can feel my gizzard shriveling deep within me as I say the next words: I want you to send me a price list so I can have boxes of your chili sent to several friends who are chili-heads of some consequence. They have always said to me, "Where, oh where, can I get chili that is *almost* as good as yours, that comes just *fairly close* to being as ambrosial as the chili you make?" And so I will tell them that, bereft of my superb chili, the next best thing they can do is order from Wick Fowler. It would be nice if you would enclose in each package an affidavit stating clearly that by ancestry, birth, education, and chili-training you are a Yankee and that through the years of your residence in Texas you have been able to fight off all efforts by citizens of that State to undermine and adulterate your chili.

Don't for god sake let Tolbert know, but I liked what the masa did for it.

Oh, what nitwits we mortals be! I was only trying to act the gentleman. What a blunder!

Several weeks after *Holiday* appeared with The Pragmatic Sanction, a lengthly article on the general subject of chili appeared in the New York *Daily News* under the byline of an old compatriot of mine, Ed Wallace. I did not, Tolbertwise, accuse Ed Wallace of being a copycat, of "borrowing freely" from me. I read his article with pleasure, for he is a man who has occasional moments of clear thinking, and his piece was wrote good. He quoted me at some length and was mildly critical of my chili theories and practices. I had no objection. I was only offended on one point. Mr. Wallace wrote:

As it turned out, fortunately, Smith has matured since I knew him as a common laborer in one of our large newspapers. Smith's piece (in *Holiday*) read quite well, made common sense, and since it was well written I knew he had composed it at least two hours after last taking food.

Reading Smith's comments and finding them risible, I recalled the words of a wise old editor in evaluating his man:

"It is hopeless to give Smith a funny piece to write immediately after he returns from lunch. For two hours he will sit there in lethargy, merely processing the news, and I will get nothing of lightness and mirth until he has slowly completed his digestion."

I do believe this dastard Wallace was hinting that I was once inclined toward middle-of-the-day boozing—an ignoble accusation, a scurrilous charge, especially in view of the fact that it is true.

As I said Mr. Wallace's article was lengthy, and there was a good deal of dross (crap) in it. His opening paragraphs may have been aimed straight at me and were loaded with illogical exposition. I choose to quote them:

> A great many men who missed their mark in life, men who played hob with all they tried to do, are not even mildly embarrassed to mask their failures by bragging that they make the greatest little pot of chili on earth.
>
> In consequence of this there is more confusion and misunderstanding on the subject of chili than surround the metric system, and more sorry opinions than becloud the making of a martini.

Manifestly, this man Wallace is a morning drinker.

And for the edification of Texans who shudder at the thought of onions chopped into chili, I set down Mr. Wallace's report on a celebrated chili-maker, the late Charlie Dressen ("The Giants is dead"), with special reference to the use of onions:

> "Onions, plenty of them there onions, that's what really makes it," Charlie once said, and whatever the remainder of the ingredients were, they must have been powerful. One sports writer, covering the Tigers during Dressen's managership, said Betty Crocker happened to read Dressen's strategy for chili con carne and was so shaken she called Ann Page and said: "Ann, come on over here and let's get drunk."

Just one more item and we'll have done with the hillbilly Wallace, taker of whisky-breaks. He reported that there was a seeming air of fear and uncertainty running through my recipe, but then good sense accumulates in his head and he continues:

> All this sounds like the work of a wish-wash chef, a man bluffing his way, but this is Smith's strength. These are the qualities that win him recognition here.
>
> Only a fool sets down precise, unalternate proportions for chili; for after a family has made chili for years and arrived at the concoction best suited to their tastes, the digestions of aging members and the teen-agers' sense of adventure, who is to say that is not the one perfect recipe for them!

The first clause of that last paragraph by Mr. Wallace was all I wanted to print, but I thought I'd include the rest of the paragraph to demonstrate how closely Mr. Wallace's literary style resembles that of the late William Faulkner.

Word reached me in Texas, too, that *Holiday* Magazine was under an avalanche of mail from its customers, most of whom were outraged by my theories about chili. Which proved the very point I made in The Pragmatic Sanction. Some of the observations about my chili, sent in by readers, went:

> . . . it isn't chili. In our family we call such atrocities "Laredo stew." It was stuff like this that killed the cowboy . . . in his attempt to escape from such gastronomic dangers he got as far as the river and couldn't make it.

Nobody knows *less* about chili than H. Allen Smith.

Smith's chili has about as much class as Automat chop suey.

His recipe wouldn't be fit to serve to a Chihuahua dog.

And so on and on—the beefs and the bellyaches were coming in at *Holiday* by the boxcarload, and they fazed me not one whit, except in the case of Maury Maverick, Jr., whose letter was a banshee wail:

> *He says he puts in one green pepper.*
> *God help us all—does he mean a bell pepper?*
> *Surely to God he didn't mean* bell *pepper!*

I began to have second thoughts about this Maury Maverick, Jr. Like his father before him this man has the reputation of being a liberal in politics, though he is clearly lacking in humanitarian instincts. I took care of his bit of griping first. There had been more hair-tearing and hoot-owl noise over that one little bitty old bell pepper than occurred after the Dempsey–Tunney fight in Philadelphia. I decided to make a sort of confession. I had never, knowingly, in all my life, put a shred of bell pepper into my chili. At the height of the bell pepper storm I sent a communiqué to the San Antonio *Express News,* a formal declaration as follows:

Dear Sir:
   I never do anything for which I have to apologize. Always, when it appears that I have committed an evil act, there are extenuating circumstances. I didn't remember that I had included bell pepper in my chili recipe in *Holiday.* Not until you and Maury Maverick called it to my attention. I confess that I did say it was okay to put in green pepper if desired.

Actually, sir, I do not believe this. It is my wife's idea. She has insisted throughout our married life that one green pepper (bell) should be chopped up and added to a pot of chili. I fought her for years but I couldn't beat her. Whenever I left out the bell pepper, she'd sneak into the kitchen, chop one up, and mix it in with my chili. I once got so desperate about this situation that I shopped all over New York for a Dutch oven equipped with a hasp and padlock (washable). I figured on getting the chili prepared and then locking the god damn pot against her, but I couldn't even find a pressure cooker with clamps that could be locked in place. A pox on the hardware trade right up to and including Hammacher-Schlemmer.

As we well know it has long been fashionable for men to work themselves to death for their women, and then leave their widows in the lap of luxury, taking world cruises, playing bridge, eating bonbons. Well, I have an intense desire to outlive my wife. I want it to be that way for one reason. It is my hope that in my final years I'll be able to make a pot of chili without a whisper of bell pepper in it.

Incidentally a transplanted New Englander named Wick Fowler, of Austin, is showering me with Texas-type chili which he manufactures, and saying nice things about my writing, and inviting me to go for a cruise on his houseboat. I suspect him of homosexual tendencies.

Yrs

H. Allen Smith

I took care of the other curmudgeons who had been writing in to *Holiday* with the following riposte:

By way of response to this flood of insolent and intemperate mail, I repeat the exact words I put into my essay: the chief ingredients of all chili are fiery envy, scalding jealousy, scorching contempt, and sizzling scorn. I entertain only the latter two emotions toward most of those who have written in.

It is clear to me that the letters coming out of our glorious Southwest, and especially out of Texas, were composed by people whose tripes have been corroded into wan and flabby whitleather by the mud-puddin' they call chili and who, in consequence, kick senior citizens and lash out at wrens.

I have little time to give to these unhappy, ill-nurtured wretches.

Two developments, however, are worth noting. A gentleman named Wick Fowler, of Austin, who has been saluted by Texans as their greatest chili cook, has sent me a case of packaged comestibles for creating his 2-Alarm Chili. Exercising great caution lest I incur permanent damage to my gizzard, I gave his product a try. I have notified him that his chili is acceptable and, in fact, is excelled only by the chili that comes out of my own kitchen. Why would I unbend so readily? Because Mr. Wick Fowler recommends tomato flavoring and onions—ingredients that have been wildly denounced by many of his Lone Star compatriots. And, secondly, because I have done some research and discovered that Mr. Fowler is a native of Presque Isle, Maine, which is as far from Texas as a man can get in the continental United States.

Moreover, I have discovered that members of the International Chili Appreciation Society salute and endorse the chili recipe of Dave Chasen, the celebrated Beverly Hills restaurant-keeper. The most dyspeptic of the Texas chili-whiners, in fact, pay compliment to Mr. Chasen's chili. It has been frozen and flown overseas in case lots to such aficionados as Elizabeth Taylor, Jimmy Stewart, and Jack Benny.

I hasten to report that Mr. Chasen's recipe calls for canned tomatoes, pinto beans *cooked in the same pot with the chili,* the very same chili powder which the Texans scorn, beef chuck that is ground coarsely, and . . . get this, please!

. . . *chopped sweet peppers.* In other words, the Dave Chasen recipe is almost a carbon copy of my own.

Take to the tules, you Lone-starred hippercrits! Let a *man* make the chili!

Returning to the matter of the bell peppers, within a very short time certain Dallas dummkopfs charged me with trying to hide behind my wife's skirts. I persuaded her, at once, to make an affidavit in which she confessed all, happily, at the same time contending that "sweet bell pepper improves every known dish with the possible exception of chocolate chiffon pie."

I do hope that I will hear no more groaning about bell peppers.

FIVE

My base of operations in Texas during this period was Alpine, a town of about 5,000 population. I intend to deal with Alpine at some length because the town occupies a prominent place in the story of The Confrontation. It comes as close to being a true cattle town as any I've seen and I've traveled a good deal in the Wild West. Real cattle ranches are scattered across Brewster County, of which Alpine is the county seat.

Many of the male citizens of Alpine affect western attire, including the cowboy hat, bush jackets, blue jeans, and high-heeled boots. They are not showing off, cutting a caper; they have a genuine liking for western clothes, and they wear them naturally. Some of them are retired ranchers, or cattlemen who prefer to direct the operations of their ranches from a comfortable house in town near the picture show and the supermarket.

The town is high and dry. It is surrounded by impressive mountain peaks and even in the hottest weeks of summer the nights are cool. As it is all over the Southwest, the major problem is water. The county gets about seventeen inches of rain a year and a lot of that evaporates in the dry atmosphere.

A story is told of a tourist approaching Mr. King Terry, a

Brewster County rancher, in the lobby of the Holland Hotel and asking him how much rain the town gets.

" 'Bout seventeen inches a year," said the rancher.

"My!" said the tourist, "that's not very much, is it?"

And Mr. King Terry said: "You oughta be here the day we git it."

Small towns in Texas, and especially in West Texas, are said to be vanishing nowadays. They can't hold the young people. Alpine survives because it has a small college—its only industry—and because of the ranchers and ex-ranchers.

I was popping in and out of Alpine with no awareness of the trouble that was brewing five hundred miles to the northeast in the daffy town of Big D, and with no awareness of the fact that eighty miles to the south was a ghost town named Terlingua where, when the sun is shining, it gets hotter than a witch's tit. In that land eighty miles is such a short distance that it's hardly worth taking the car; might as well walk it. It's too bad I didn't know about Terlingua; it's too bad I had no inkling of the fact that Terlingua would very shortly bulk large in my life. I could have strolled down there after supper some evening and done a bit of preliminary scouting and worked out some strategical and tactical things. There can be no understanding of a mighty conflict like The Confrontation, no adequate planning of war, without a knowledge of the terrain. I must point out, however, that I was not real terribly handicapped by ignorance of the Terlingua neighborhood. Other warriors have gone into battle as ignorantly. I'm quite sure that Stonewall Jackson, a West Virginia boy, knew very little about life in the village of Chancellorsville (where *he* got *his*).

I know very little about the science of military strategy, though I'm aware of the fact that we should never think of strategy as a positivistic science. I never do. Nonetheless I have looked into the theories of Liddell Hart, with special reference to Napoleon's maneuverings, the operations of

Marlborough, of Maurice de Saxe, of Turenne, and of the elder von Moltke. I have boned up on Scipio Africanus Major who conquered Hannibal at Zama—but he was a hateful old bastard and weak-headed in the bargain, believing himself to be divinely inspired; I have no use for his kind of strategy.

I have a feeling that I knew less about strategy in the end than I did when I began investigating it and even if I had become skilled in the military arts, I don't know what good they would have done me at Terlingua. Only one shot was fired there, and it was not heard round the world; to this day nobody knows who fired it.

I prefer to play around with the literary stratagem of the diversionary, tangential digression. I was walking along the main street of Alpine one afternoon and suddenly I spoke to myself, saying, "What in the name of Christ am I doing out here in Alpine, Texas?" I thought about the question for a few moments and then something came back to me. I went over to the Alpine Public Library and found a book called *We Went Thataway*, which I had written twenty years earlier. It is a small travel masterpiece and the town of Alpine appears in it, as follows:

> Alpine is a small town in West Texas and we drove straight through it and were a couple of miles east of it when I pulled up at the side of the road and remarked that there was something about the place that appealed to me. We turned around and went back and found a fairly large hotel called the Holland.
>
> The man at the desk said, "You huntin' antelope?"
>
> "No," I said.
>
> He examined some papers and then announced that we were lucky.
>
> "Hunt's on," he said, "but a bird from Dallas knocked over a doe 'smornin' and just left in disgrace. You can have his room."

Up to this time I had little or no interest in the antelope. I had at my fingertips just one single fact concerning the animal, and I hadn't possessed it very long. Back in South Dakota someone told me that an antelope has an unusual behind. The rump of the antelope is white and in ordinary circumstances nice-looking, if you go for rumps. Under excitement, however, the antelope's bottom *expands to twice its normal size*. Let a hunter come over a hill and swoosh! the antelope's behind explodes outward in all directions, and away he goes. This mechanism was arranged by Nature; the expanded rump is a flag of warning to other antelope, telling them to floss out their own and start running.

At first I thought a little sadly on the fact that Nature hadn't given human beings this same characteristic. Actually I wouldn't want to have such a thing happening to me, much as I would enjoy seeing it in other people. Suppose under fear or excitement our posteriors flared out to twice their normal size. I know some people it would knock to the ground. We'd all have to wear rubber pants. The close-fitting chair would go out of fashion, else there would be occasions even at polite gatherings where the room would be full of flying chair rungs. Think of the things that might happen in a crowded subway car. Maybe it's just as well that this function is confined to the antelope.

By chance we had arrived in Alpine in the middle of a three-day antelope hunt, and the Holland Hotel was headquarters for the operation. As for Alpine itself, one of its citizens described it as "the biggest city in the biggest county in the biggest State in the Union." It is surrounded by cattle ranches and the owners of these ranches congregate in the lobby of the Holland. Some of them, retired from active direction of their cattle empires, sit there all day in the leather chairs and talk cow talk. And quite a few men in Alpine tote guns.

We got acquainted with the manager of the hotel and pumped him for information. What distinction did Alpine enjoy beyond the antelope hunt? He mentioned a baseball team and a college football team, but the town's biggest brag is this:

"Only one man was ever convicted of murder in this county, and he was an outsider. Came up here from Harlingen and dropped some kid off a mountain to collect the insurance. Somehow that didn't set well with the people around here. You can steal a cow and get yourself in plenty of trouble. Nobody's going to mind it much if you kill somebody—but don't drop no kid off no mountain."

When the hotel man asked how we liked our room I said it was satisfactory but why was it in western hotels that the beds are seldom equipped with lights for reading?

"It's been tried," he said, "but it doesn't work. People out here, no matter whether they're ranchers or drummers, they go to bed to sleep, not to read. You fix a light at the head of a bed and right away you start getting complaints —they say they're always bangin' their heads against the damn things."

The mechanics of Alpine's antelope hunt are intricate. It all begins in the State capital at Austin with the announcement of the date when for three days it will be legal to shoot buck antelope in Brewster County. Applications are in order. More than ten thousand hunters including a few women apply for licenses. Meanwhile the Game and Fish Department has decided that only five hundred and ninety-two hunters will be given permits to shoot one antelope each in Brewster County. So the ten thousand applications are put in a bowl and five hundred and ninety-two are drawn out. The winners are then notified. Each of them sends in twenty-five dollars, and the licenses are mailed to them together with instructions.

While all this is going on in Austin the owners of ranches in Brewster County are advising the authorities whether they'll permit hunters on their land during the three days. A rancher is required to designate the exact number of hunters that will be permitted on his property.

Thus each hunter is informed by mail that he is to report on a certain day at the Holland Hotel in Alpine and make contact with the party which has been assigned to do its hunting on, say, the Gage Holland ranch.

Two days before the start of the slaughter the hunters come swarming into the hotel. Arriving at the same time are the masters of the hunt—a troop of about three hundred game wardens. On the morning of the first day the hotel is alive with activity as early as four o'clock. Cavalcades of automobiles, led by game wardens, go roaring out of town in all directions. A rough time is in store for the beautiful flare-butted antelope.

Each hunter is permitted to kill one buck, and he has three days to do the job. Most of them get their antelope the first day, return to the hotel, drink a toast in straight bourbon, pack up, and leave for home. Some go three days without success. And some go away in disgrace for having killed a doe by mistake.

One of Alpine's leading citizens is Cas Edwards, who writes occasional pieces for the magazines, who is a naturalist of sorts, a poet, historian, and author of a little book called *Cowboy Philosophy*. Mr. Edwards sat in the hotel lobby with me and observed the frenzied comings and goings of the antelope hunters and answered questions about the economics of the sport.

It works out something like this: a man's name is drawn from the bowl in Austin, and he pays twenty-five dollars for his license, provided he lives in Texas; if he is an out-of-state hunter he antes up five hundred dollars. Now he has to pay his transportation to Alpine and his hotel bill, and his equipment and clothing are usually expensive. The customary fee paid to the rancher on whose land he is assigned to hunt is one hundred dollars. Those are the basic charges. If he happens to kill a doe he is subject to a fine; if he kills a buck there is considerable expense involved in having it dressed and shipped back home.

Why does he do it? I suggested to Cas Edwards that shooting antelope must be great sport. Why wasn't *he* out there with them?

"Around here," he said, "we never go after antelope.

Don't believe in it. No sport to it at all. It's like shootin' a lady. It's like shootin' a milk-pen calf. An antelope is a purty thing. Got sad and soulful eyes. They say an antelope is smart, because he'll sometimes just stand and stare at a hunter. They say when he's standin' there he's sizin' up his man, he's even countin' the cattridges in the gun to see what the odds are against him. They say he's got a lot of curiosity in him, and that all a man has to do is act crazy and the antelope will come toward him. There are some hunters who lay down on their backs and stick their feet up in the air and wiggle them and poke their gun barrel between their legs. The minute they do that and the antelope sees them, that antelope gets curious about what the hell is goin' on. So he keeps comin' closer, peerin' at the guy on the ground, and pretty soon he comes close enough so the guy can shoot between his legs and bring him down."

"Well," I said, "if it's not good sport, then why do they come all the way down here and spend all that money?"

Mr. Edwards got out of his chair and motioned for me to follow him. He led me across the lobby to the corridor and pointed to the mounted head of an antelope on the wall.

"That's what they're after," he said. "The head. That's the whole story. All they want is the head so they can have it mounted and stick it up in their livin' room and spend the rest of their days talkin' about it, braggin' about it. Sometimes I think they're loco."

The retired ranchers who sit in the Holland lobby want no part of foreigners and whenever I tried to ease myself into their conversations their eyes told me to mosey. Then someone suggested that if I approached one of them, a heavyset man with spectacular jowls, and spoke the name of Calvin Coolidge, I might get some action. When the moment seemed propitious I dropped into a chair beside him and said, "Are you the man who knew Coolidge?"

"*Knew* him!" he exploded. "I didn't know him. But I called him a-plenty, the sour-pussed son of a bitch, and I hope he heard me."

"What did you call him?" I asked. "What happened?"

"Well, his train come through here that day and stopped down at the depot. All the school children were down there, and that dumb son of a bitch didn't even look at them. Walked out on that platform and looked right over their heads. We had a Chamber of Commerce fella here, young man, up and jumpin', full of piss and vinegar. Well, he had got up a portfolio of beautiful pictures of our mountains to give to the President as a gift. He climbed up on the platform and held the portfolio out, and that mean son of a bitch wouldn't take it. I'd have hit him with a rock, regardless of who he was. I was back there in the crowd and saw the whole thing, and I spoke up loud. I said, 'Hit the dumb son of a bitch with it, boy!' and I said, 'It's no wonder this country's in the shape it's in, with a dumb son of a bitch like that at the head of the gov'ment.' I said it so he could hear it, and I think he did, and I hope he did, the dumb son of a bitch."

Along about this time my wife came back from a walk around the streets of Alpine, and when we were alone she asked me if I had ever had my car snappered.

"Snappered?" I repeated. "Not that I know of. Never heard of it. What is it?"

It came as no surprise to me that Texans have their cars snappered now and then. Here as elsewhere there are plenty of regional peculiarities and folkways. We had learned already that Texans scorn the use of paper book matches, that drugstores carry suction kits containing equipment for treating rattlesnake bites, that many Texans use a pencil when they write a check.

"I noticed," said my wife, "a place here in town where they snapper your car. Must be some kind of special servicing job."

"Maybe they put snappers on your clutch," I suggested.

"What are snappers?" she asked.

"How the hell should I know?"

We went about our business, but I couldn't get rid of it—it was one of those things that wiggle around in your mind, refusing to go away. Finally I told her I thought she had a froze brain. "You can get a car greased," I said, "and washed and painted and simonized, but not snappered."

"All right, Mr. Wise Guy," she said, "you know everything. It's right up the street here. Come on. I'll show you."

We walked a short distance, and she pointed to a filling station, and there it was, a big sign that said "*Snapper Service.*" Probably because she had built the thing up it took me a few moments to catch on. Then I realized what it meant—the place was operated by some people named Snapper.

There was a football game in town that evening, and we soon learned that everyone in Alpine was going to attend it. Fifteen minutes before kickoff time there wasn't a soul in the hotel lobby except for the night clerk, and along the main street all the stores were dark despite the fact that it was Saturday night. The little movie house had its marquee lights twinkling, but we saw no customers going in. So we hopped in the car and drove over to the field and found seats in the stand. The local teachers' college was playing somebody—I can't even remember the name of the invading force. It was a runaway for the Alpines. All through the first half they scored at will. The way it looked to me, the visitors were so clumsy and inept that the Alpine boys could make a touchdown any time they felt like it. So when the half ended I decided I had seen enough.

"Lousy football," I said. "Let's get out of here. These people don't know anything about the game."

It wasn't until a month later when we were back home that I learned we had been watching one of the greatest football teams of the entire Southwest. The local teachers' college in Alpine was Sul Ross, and that team went through the season undefeated, and its backfield stars were among the nation's top scorers and played in one of the bowl games. And I walked out on them at the half. . . .

In Alpine we began to acquire an awareness of the fact that Texans regard their State not only as a country in itself, but a world in itself. At that football game just as we reached our seats the school band paraded onto the field, went into position facing the crowd, and everyone stood up. The men removed their hats and placed them over their hearts and those without hats placed their hands there. I waited for the opening bars of the "Star-Spangled Banner" but they didn't come. Instead the band played "I've Been Workin' on the Railroad." This is unofficially the Texas anthem, and when it is played strong men bow their heads and sometimes make a silent vow to destroy Oklahoma. The tune is the railroad song, but the words are different, and the anthem is called "The Eyes of Texas Are Upon You." This was a phrase used frequently years ago by the president of the young university at Austin. Apparently his students were not too interested in education, so he would remind them now and then that the eyes of Texas were upon them. One day when they were getting up a campus minstrel show they decided to poke some fun at the prexy's nagging cry concerning the eyes of Texas. They used the railroad tune and wrote new words, and a joke became an anthem, and today if you are in Texas and hear that music and don't get to your feet you're likely to be jerked there.

I remember asking the hotel manager in Alpine where all the antelope hunters came from. "They're from all over the country," he said. Subsequently I learned that he meant they were from all over Texas. And it was in Alpine that an elderly citizen disappeared for a couple of weeks, and when he turned up someone asked him where he had been.

"Been travelin'," he said.

"Where'd you go?"

"Went as fur East as I could git without gittin' outa the country."

"New York?"

"Corpus," he said.

Later in that same book written more than twenty years ago, just before leaving the State in my flying saucer, I rendered an opinion about Texas and the Texans. I think it is appropriate that I reprint it here:

Texas brags and the rest of the country whines about it. Those of us who do the whining are, I think, more at fault than the talking Texans. I got terribly tired of listening to them yammer about the glories of their State. The underlying reason for my irritation was this: they say they've got the biggest this and the most that and the goldarndest this and the rip-snortin'est that, and they go on and on with it —and the maddening thing about it is: *they really got it.*

They've got everything. We saw only a small portion of their empire (nobody has ever seen it all), yet we looked at every known kind of scenery except icebergs. They've got deserts and craggy mountains and jungles and swamps and vast prairies and fertile farmlands and seaports. They've got every kind of weather from hurricanes to blinding heat to tornadoes to chilling northers to sub-zero blizzards. They've got cities that will probably outstrip Chicago before very long. They have their own anthem and their own flag, and while we were in San Antonio the newspapers announced with eight-column banner lines that Texas was reorganizing her own Navy—seven vessels, donated by private citizens. They are as friendly to the visitor as any people on earth so long as the visitor doesn't begin telling them what they ought to do. They want "foreigners" to like them. I think the rest of us should admire them and respect them because, after all, they won the war—World War II. Told me so themselves.

SIX

Out in Dallas this Frank X. Tolbert continued studying my recipe for chili as set forth in *Holiday*, slavering over the splendid sound of it, but out of weird misguided loyalties he continued his attack on me. He used his column to sound off in hemidemisemithunderous undertones. A sort of squeak.

He called my beautiful recipe "a chili-powder flavored, low-torque beef gruel" and began referring to me as "Soupy" Smith. He dispatched an appeal to Wick Fowler in Austin. Mr. Fowler rolled out of his steerhide hammock, yawned, burped melodiously, scratched himself, turned coat (as Maury Maverick was doing), and allowed that my chili was on the sissy side.

"The maternity wards in Texas hospitals," said Mr. Fowler, "have to warm up Smith's formula before feeding it to newborn babies." Quite palpably this man, who had been friendly in the beginning, did not realize the gravity of the matter at hand. I knew, without ever having met him, that he was a clunk.

The troglodytic X. Tolbert never let up, and Mr. Fowler himself enlisted the yellow journals of Austin and San Antonio in the dissemination of calumny. They made sport of my initials, calling me "ole H. A." and sometimes "that ole H. A." Penny-a-liner Tolbert quoted his readers as saying such things as "Why don't he just eat clabber?" and "I know him—he's the one puts sugar in his martinis."

I felt that I had become a mere pawn in the dog-eat-dog of chili appreciation. Newspapers all over Texas began sniping at me. It became the fashion to refer to me as "a book writer," making an epithet out of the phrase, giving it a tone which implied that writing a book is an onanistic pursuit. All I had done was to utter a clean conservative statement of fact—the simple declaration that Texas chili is slop that would sicken a water buffalo. A plain sentiment that offended and even enraged a lot of Texans.

At one point I found myself reflecting on the career of a tender-hearted road agent named John Judkin Hodges who, brought to book on a charge of robbing a stage, heard the court clerk in Fort Davis intone: "The People of the State of Texas against John Judkin Hodges." The defendant passed a hand across his eyes and murmured: "Lord God, what a majority!" My own feelings exactly.

A package came to my home, a package containing a book and a note from Wick Fowler. The book was titled *With or Without Beans,* and had been written by a Texan named Joe E. Cooper, a newspaperman turned press agent, born in a Texas Bethlehem (the little town of Midlothian, south of Dallas) and destined to become the patron saint of the Chili Appreciation Society International and author of The Scripture (as his book is called). The book's subtitle is "An Informal Biography of Chili" and it was published by a Texas firm. Wick Fowler suggested that if I really felt like learning the basic facts about chili I should put in a few days of diligent study of The Scripture. I put in part of one day. When I had finished with it I knew that chili in Texas is not a comestible. Chili in Texas is a religion. Orthodox. If I may enlarge upon this judgment, let me say that I would soon learn that Texans are greedy for two things: chili and money. For a while I thought their greed for chili was dominant, but I was to find out through personal experience that their greed for money is obsessive—the same as it is elsewhere, though I do believe the Texas appetite is more voracious than in any other clime where I have lived or visited. They go clean out of their heads at the mere thought of a greenback. Yes . . . Texans can hold their heads high with pride when it comes to greed.

One thing in The Scripture gave me pleasure—the revelation that Texans are by no means agreed on chili. They quibble and quarrel among themselves worse than the Guelphs and the Ghibellines, a classical allusion. In Joe E. Cooper's book there are cited more ways to confect chili than there are sexual perversions known to modern civilized man. It surprised me that Mr. Cooper hadn't included a recipe which appeared in a weekly newspaper in my town of Mount Kisco, a recipe for "chili con tuna." I rag you not. That recipe all but destroyed any affection I might have had for the town.

The Texas chili cult is a religion as surely as there are Texas Holy Rollers and Texas Baptists. Members of the Chili Appreciation Society International, for example, open their meetings with holy rites. I have not attended any of their sessions, having no more desire to congregate with them than I have to congregate with platoons of Brownies. But I have heard that they begin the proceedings with a wand drill—a thing that seems unlikely, because every public function of any kind in Texas opens with prayer. A report also reached me that after the cracker-breaking ceremony at a CASI orgy, pins are stuck into images of those of us who put tomatoes in chili and eschew cornmeal. I have no doubt that other forms of incantation, conjurement, shamanism, and hex-working are practiced by the Dallas Fairy Circle.

In The Scripture Joe E. Cooper calls them "chilicrats." A quote from his book serves the CASI for a motto: "The aroma of good chili should generate rapture akin to a lover's kiss." The pages are loaded with suchlike reverent observations. For example, The Prophet speaks several times of the fact that the late Admiral Chester Nimitz, a native of Fredericksburg, always saved out enough chili from his evening meal to pour over his eggs at next morning's breakfast.

In the early pages of The Scripture the overall tone is set by Charles Pettit, a prominent Texas rancher, who demonstrates how the average Texan can go daft just thinking about chili. Cow Fellow Pettit, it seems, distributes calendars with the following tender message:

> Chili . . . is found only in the Western Continent and only in parts of it. It long has existed but has been used by relatively few. Columbus heard of it and came to America looking for it. Ponce de Leon was hunting for it when we first heard of him down in Florida. De Soto was in search of it when he crossed the Mississippi. Washington and his men had some of it, then they ferried the Brandywine. Stonewall Jackson had a good deal of it. Sam Houston took what chili Santa Anna had at San Jacinto. Hitler got a little bit, but evidently didn't give any to his army. Stalin has heard about it and is looking for it.

There is a statement by General Ike Ashburn, who was publisher of the magazine *Texas Parade*, in which he sets himself up as a man with an intense liking for chili. He tells of having had New Year's Day dinner at the home of his sister in Greenville, consuming great quantities of baked ham, roast beef, turkey, plum pudding, and boiled custard. Right after dinner the menfolks went downtown to the post office and General Ashburn stopped off at the depot to watch the Katy limited come in. When the other men found him he was at the counter in Brother Jonathan's eating emporium wolfing down a bowl of red.

The religious overtones of the chili crowd are reflected in many chapters and verses of The Scripture. Speculations about the origin of chili often contain broad hints that a miracle was wrought. One, for example, tells how a Mexican cook in a cow camp ran out of black pepper and, as a sort of desperate measure to keep the cowboys from beating his butt off, put some of his private stock of red chiles in his son-of-a-bitch stew, thus starting up chili and drawing huzzahs from the waddies.

It must be noted, too, that for years there has been theological disputation on the editorial pages of Texas newspapers over the ordained way of spelling the word *chili,* or *chile.* It seems to have escaped everybody that a simple rule might govern the matter. Chili, the dish, is chili in the United States of America. Chile, the pepper, is chile everywhere. Thus a good bowl of chili is made good by the inclusion of macerated chile.°

The fact, however, that I was dealing with a religion, that I was challenging a religion, didn't disturb me a bit and I never pulled a punch on account of it. I am unchurched and nonholy and even the mightiest of the preachers fail to frighten me.

I must confess, however, that my reading of The Scripture furnished me with some fragments of knowledge which I didn't possess before. I didn't know that most domestic chili powder includes in its composition other basic flavorings than chile itself. I always assumed that chili powder was made from straight chiles, but now I learned that most manufacturers include cumin and oregano and perhaps salt and maybe garlic powder and a little monosodium glutimate in their product. I don't necessarily believe what I read in any scriptures, so I checked around and verified this. If you are

° Some Texas monsters, cited in The Scripture, spell it "chilly." In 1968 an Illinois newspaper put out a wordy supplement supporting the claim that Springfield is the true chili capital of the world. The dumbhead newspaper in my home State destroyed its own argument by spelling it "chilli." I've never encountered people who can, on occasion, be as dumb as the people of Illinois.

fortunate enough to have access to chili powder without the other flavorings mixed into it, you should use greater quantities of cumin and garlic and oregano. And once again let me emphasize that creating a bowl of chili is much the same as painting a landscape or writing a novel—you make it up as you go along rather than follow prescribed regulations imposed by dictators who write cook books.

Reading Joe Cooper's holy writ, I got the impression that Texas men have tried to simulate a lot of the *machismo* that is characteristic of the Mexican male; *machismo* is the Mexican principle of maleness, masculinity, super-potency, self-cocking virility. A Mexican gentleman in the deep autumn years of his life, afflicted with rickets, general softening of the bones, and Parkinson's disease, will contend that he is twice as good with the ladies as any milksop gringo. Texas gentlemen exhibit much the same immaturity in their incessant clamoring for hotter and hotter and still hotter chili. A Texan, says the Cooper Good Book, wants his chili hot enough to kill knee-high cotton. I might interpolate, at this point, a quote I once copied out of a book by Erna Fergusson of New Mexico; Miss Fergusson was in turn quoting somebody in Mexico on the subject of chile—the hot pepper, not the bowl of red—which "protects against colds and malaria, it aids digestion, it clarifies the blood, it develops robustness and resistance to the elements; it even acts as a stimulant to the romantically inclined." I would suspect that Miss Fergusson was setting down words spoken by a Texan, except for the fact that a Texan would never say he needed chile to elevate his romantic inclinations. A few months ago a UPI dispatch came out of Jalapa in Mexico* telling of Francisco Evarardo Cruz Hernandez and his 102nd birthday party. He said he was able to reach that age

* The celebrated *chiles jalapeños* come from Jalapa. I once visited a plant there where they can the *jalapeños* and carried away half a case. They are among the world's finest vegetables.

because he ate a lot of stuffed chiles, or *chiles rellenos*. It is my guess that he also bragged about sacking out the night before with a teen-age senorita.

Hot-pepper *machismo* among the Texans is reflected in The Scripture by such recurring phrases as "hot enough to scald a hog" and "hot enough to make the toenails slip." A man named Wally Boren is quoted as having said that chili is a stew that can "sit on a cold stove and boil gently."

This kind of scriptural talk is undiluted crap. I have been manufacturing *salsa picante*, the universal Mexican sauce, in my home for years. It can be made wild and it can be made tame. In Mexico *salsa* is always on the table, three meals a day, the way the English keep a pot of mustard close at hand at all times. (American tourists always say the English use mustard to kill the taste of their drab and dreary cookery. American tourists say it, I don't.) In Westchester County, New York, I have for a long time raised my own chiles. I used these New York grown chiles to make *salsa*. It is a simple procedure and if you have a leaning toward hot, spicy things, you ought to know how to do it. It can be made with any kind of hot peppers; cherry peppers will do, or the long yellow Hungarian variety which are available in jars in many stores. The Hungarian are about the mildest of all *picante* peppers and I know a doctor named Rusher who sits around gnawing on them as if they were bananas.

Now: Take the seeds out of the peppers. If you enjoy a lot of strength, leave the veins in—otherwise pare them out. Chop the peppers and chop an equal amount of onion and tomato—fresh tomato if available, canned tomatoes if needs be. Add minced garlic if you feel like it, and salt. Mix this all together, put it in a jar—I generally make a quart at a time —and store it in the refrigerator. It will keep a long time. Mix a spoonful of *salsa* into eggs before scrambling, or sprinkle some on fried eggs; use it in soups and stews and as a side-dressing for any kind of meat—use it with everything but ice cream. I wouldn't be without it. Some of the girl editors at the *Reader's Digest*, near my home, were daffy for *salsa* and I used to make up extra batches and keep them supplied; they spread the word and gave other girl editors samplings and before long the demands upon me were so great that I either had to set up a *salsa* factory or turn my back on the ladies. I turned my back on the ladies. *Salsa*wise only.*

As stated you may vary your proportions to suit the toughness or tenderness of your mouth. I have a tough mouth for fiery comestibles, yet I have encountered people who could out-tough me by forty furlongs. Once in Mexico City I came upon handsome Peaches Guerrero of Honolulu nibbling on some tiny chiles. She offered one to me and I took it happily and bit into it and started chewing. The whole interior of my head caught fire, there were throbbing pains and clanking noises; tears coursed down my face and I gasped and gurgled and gagged like a man dying in agony. That's the way it goes with our friend the chile. I know people who undergo the same convulsions at my table when they have a try at my *salsa*.

There are some good things in The Scripture. By "good" I mean interesting things to know. The book contains 242 pages and includes observations and opinions from dozens of men and a few women. For example, there are several degenerate Texans who actually advocate the use of gristle in chili. They *call for it*. This is an abomination that sickens

---

* In Alpine and Brewster County people put *salsa* on their tables but they call it *chile macho*. When I refer to it as *salsa*, they contemplate me as if I were a toadfrog. The correct name is *salsa*. I wondered where they got *chile macho*, and asked Phyllis Connor of Alpine. She said *macho* is a term for a little horse, and that the sauce is called *chile macho* "because it makes you prance and jump around." I have written elsewhere about how Ginny Street grew fond of my *salsa* and began making it in her own home; she could never remember the word for it, so she undertook memory-by-association. She always thought of alka salsa.

me. I spend more time trimming my meat, or supervising its trimming, than I do at any other stage of the proceedings. On the other hand Joe E. Cooper quotes a few Texans who complain about some restaurant chili and some canned chili as having "too much" gristle. God damn it to hell, there should be NO gristle. I am so violently opposed to gristle that I wouldn't feed it to a starving dog, or an affectionate saber-toothed tiger.

The Wally Boren quoted a few paragraphs back appears again in the book with a proposal which I am inclined to endorse. "It ought to be illegal," he said, "to label that unstrained catsup stuff as chili sauce. The word chili should be applied only to the genuine article." This takes me back to 1929 when I first went to New York from Denver, a good chili town. I wanted chili and I couldn't conceive of the Greatest City on Earth being without it. I used to go in the grocery stores and delicatessens and ask, "You got any chili?" In every case the clerk would come up with a bottle of the aforementioned unstrained catsup stuff, which unnerved and aggravated me to such an extent that all during the succeeding forty years I have had no traffic with the unstrained catsup stuff.

Finally, the CASI gospel according to Joe Cooper has this to say in its consideration of chili history: "A majority of those who hold for Texas origin fasten it to the brush country of Southwest Texas where cowhands lived long stretches out of the grub box of a chuck wagon, and where stinted home cooks fed families with whatever came to hand."

Poppy J. Cock! Southwest Texas is the part of Texas I like best and I'd enjoy knowing that chili had its origin there. But it didn't. The hell with holy writ. Chili originated in San Antonio. Period.

SEVEN

In the pages of The Scripture are many recipes for making chili, some of them bordering on absurdity, some others being the dream-patterns of lunatics. On the other hand, there just had to be a few of them that made sense. I want to present a couple to those of you who are inclined, as I am, toward experimentation. Chili is not a religion with me—I am not fundamentalist about it. Therefore I offer these two recipes as being fun to fool around with.

The first comes from the kitchen of the late E. DeGolyer, a world traveler, a gourmet, a litterateur, a sense-making citizen of Dallas, and a gentleman. Mr. DeGolyer was first known to me as proprietor of the *Saturday Review of Literature* in New York and in those years I was not aware of his reputation as "the Solomon of the chili bowl." He not only loved chili, he spent a lot of time delving into chili history and chili lore. In the end he arrived at a formula that suited his taste perfectly; if you have the time and the inclination give Chili DeGolyer a try. It goes this way:

3 pounds center cut steak. Trim and cut into cubes of less than one-half-inch dimension. Lazy people grind meat in a food chopper using only the coarse knife.

2½ cups of fat rendered from beef suet.

2 to 12 pods of *chile colorado,* or dried peppers, according to taste. If you are *muy fuerte,* use more.

2 cups of water or the liquid in which the *chiles* have been boiled.

4 cloves chopped garlic.

1 onion, chopped.

1 teaspoon comino seeds (cumin in English, or kummel if you understand it better).

1 teaspoon oregano (marjoram).

1 tablespoon salt.

Brown onion and garlic in fat, add meat, and cook until gray (not brown) in color.

Add 2 cups of water and let simmer for an hour.

Take pods of dried *chile,* wash, stem, and remove seeds. Take care with the seeds for, as your Chronicler says, "that which is sharp and biting . . . be the veins and grains only, the rest is not." Put to boil in cold water and boil slowly until skins slip easily, usually three-quarters of an hour. When you have become expert you roast the pods instead of boiling. In either event rub the pulp through a colander or sieve to make a smooth paste. You should now have a half to three-quarters of a cup of pulp.

Chili powder, prepared commercially, may be substituted for the pulp at the equivalent of one heaping tablespoon of chili powder for two pods of chile. The flavor is never as delicate but you can avoid the chile burn that results from too much handling of that aggressive vegetable.*

Rub comino seeds and oregano to a powder, toasting if need be. Add chile pulp, comino, oregano powder, and salt to the meat and cook slowly for an hour.

---

* The first year that I grew my own chiles in Westchester County I made a mistake. I harvested my first batch and in the kitchen trimmed them, removing seeds and veins, *barehanded.* My fingers burned for ten days, and I couldn't sleep nights because of the fire in my hands. Thereafter I used rubber gloves whenever I handled hot peppers.

Now, my friends, I had great respect for Brother De-Golyer but I think his operation is somewhat like crocheting a rug for the lobby of the Waldorf. I have gone through the whole procedure, using chili powder instead of the pods, and it is fine chili, *special* chili, chili for showing off. But my god it's a lot of work!

The second recipe out of The Scripture is from the hand of The Prophet himself. This is Joe E. Cooper's way with chili:

3 pounds lean beef.
¼ cup olive oil.
1 quart water.
2 bay leaves (if desired).
8 dry chile pods, OR 6 tablespoons chili powder.
3 teaspoons salt.
10 cloves finely chopped garlic.
1 teaspoon ground comino.
1 teaspoon oregano (marjoram).
1 teaspoon red pepper.
½ teaspoon black pepper.
1 tablespoon sugar.
3 tablespoons paprika.
3 tablespoons flour.
6 tablespoons cornmeal.

When olive oil is hot, in 6-quart pot, add meat and sear over high heat; stir constantly until gray—NOT BROWN. It will then have consistence of whole-grain hominy. Add one quart water and cook (covered) at bubbling simmer one and one-half to two hours.

Add all ingredients except thickening. Cook 30 minutes longer at same bubbling simmer. Further cooking will damage some of the spice flavors. Now add thickening, previously mixed in cold water. Cook five minutes to determine if more water is necessary (likely) for your desired consistency. Stir to prevent sticking after thickening is added.

Some prefer all flour, others all cornmeal, and still others use cracker meal—about as good, and more convenient. Suit your own taste.

If you like bay flavor (it is good) 2 leaves for 15/20 minutes at start. They'll be easier to find, for removal, before spices are added.

In case much fat was left in meat, it will show on top after spices are added. Too much suet in chili produces unpleasant backfires. You'll find out how much to keep by experience.

Pepper indicated will make fairly hot chili—about average. A first-timer might start with less and taste his. . . .

Oh, hell! I can't go on with this farce any longer! Throughout this chili controversy I have been a sportsman, fair, honorable. I've functioned with a keen sense of justice and probity. I have not lost my temper. I have not indulged in personalities. But these Texans are guilty of foolishness worse confounded. I'm sorry to have to say so, but that Cooper recipe demonstrates just how vulnerable, and how idiotic, religious leaders can be.

You want good chili, do it *my* way.

EIGHT

It is difficult for me to keep up with my correspondence and business affairs when I am off traveling, yet I have to do it because of my worldwide reputation as a 20th-century Renaissance Man, a dynamic dilettante in two dozen fascinating fields of endeavor. *

I've forgotten where I had paused in my wanderings around South Texas and west of the Pecos when I got word from my New York agent that I had been challenged to a duel. Wick Fowler of Austin had flung down the gauntlet and offered to cook chili against me anytime, anywhere, under any rules. I responded that I would not be drawn into combat with trash. Fowler, in collaboration with the varlet X. Tolbert, launched a torrent of abuse against me, charging me with arrant chickenhood, saying that I had taken to my bed with the Buff Orpington syndrome. I was in a fury; my deep fealty to the middle western concept of chili had been wounded; the storied honor of the Illinois Smiths had been impugned. I fumed, but I still hesitated. . . .

I had been corresponding on another matter with Wayne Sargent, a vice-president of United Press International, a

---

* For evidence in support of this statement, see the character called H. Allen Smith in the fine novel, *Son of Rhubarb,* published by Trident Press in 1967. Live a little.

74

man who had spent some time in Dallas and other parts of Texas. I told him of the challenge, and he counseled me: "Face up to them. They are not much. Most of them have a strong streak of masochism. They like to suffer. Their wives pick on them. Their kids pick on them. To round out their miserable day they'll cook that junk and eat it and holler, 'Boy, that's good chili!' It is not good chili. It is owl residue. Go and cook."

There was something reassuring and comforting, encouraging, and even inspirational in Mr. Sargent's penultimate observation. Emboldened now, I notified X. Tolbert that if I could locate a horsewhip I was coming to Dallas and horsewhip him in front of his colleagues of the Dallas *News*. I added that as long as I would have to pay for the airline fare, it would be my pleasure while in Dallas to horsewhip everyone else in that city who pretends to a knowledge of chili.

"It is often said," I wrote, "that if you look long enough you can find, somewhere in New York City, any article or product that exists all around the world. For several days I have been searching diligently for a horsewhip and I haven't been able to find one. It seems a shame that the venerable institution, once so popular in America, of the indignant subscriber horsewhipping an editor, has altogether vanished. We are growing soft. I am not a subscriber to the Dallas *News* and I don't think you are technically an editor. Still, as soon as I find a horsewhip I'm going to climb on a plane and come down there and horsewhip you at your desk."

Soon I had a brisk reaction from other Texas newspapermen. Mayo Lanagan of Lone Star wrote suggesting that I also horsewhip Sam Paris, who commands the night desk at the Longview *Morning Journal*, though Mr. Lanagan's reasons were unclear. Another Texas journalist, whose letter I misplaced, shipped me a beautiful Mexican whip, made of braided black and white leather, which he said would be nice to use on Tolbert's hide. He also sent me a list of twenty-three other Texas newspapermen and asked me to horsewhip each of them good while I was at it.

To Mr. Lanagan I wrote:

Dear Mr. Lanagan:

Why don't you stay out of this horsewhipping campaign of mine?

The very first paragraph of your letter to the chili-spoiler Tolbert shows the extent of your ignernts. You say that I proposed to whip Tolbert "before God and everybody else in the Dallas *News* office." If you knew anything at all, you'd know that God has never been near the Dallas *News*. The religious editor of that paper, I hear, is a Rosicrucian on the verge of apostasizing to Jehovah's Other Witnesses. I hear they will turn him down and then he'll have to go through with his plan to form a new cult, the Eighth Day Adventists.

Is Longview anywhere near Lone Star? If I go to all the trouble to horsewhip Sam Paris, I'd want to raise a few welts on *your* shoulder blades while I was at it. Bleed you up a little. Teach you respect for northern intellectuals. I would want to charge admission to the horsewhipping of both you and Sam Paris. Dollar a head. That's what I hear they are getting for authenticated cow flops from the LBJ ranch.

Yrs

H. Allen Smith

Under the threat of a horsewhipping, X. Tolbert quailed and, seeking to mollify me, invited me to "the gala autumn orgy and fertility rites of the Society in Dallas." I declined on the grounds that I had an earlier engagement—I was going to Edna Ferber's home to cook a pot of my fine chili for her.

The CASI response was to install a garbage can at the head table with my name on it.

X. Tolbert grew so choleric that he almost forgot to drag the name of J. Frank Dobie into the controversy; such an oversight is the equivalent, in Texas, of expectorating on the Alamo. But Tolbert now quoted Dobie—I've forgotten the context—and I was able to stun him with one of Dobie's own parables: a cowboy entered a Texas restaurant, took note of the dirt on the floor, on the table, on the ceiling, on the waiter, and said, "All I want is a coconut and a hammer."

I figured it was about time for all this tumult and shouting to die away and so I traveled down to a mining village called La Linda, on the Mexican shore of the Rio Grande south of Marathon, a settlement ruled over by a large Texan named Gene Morgan. I stayed in a comfortable ranch house on the American side of the river, with a Mexican cook and a Mexican male maid, and I tried to get a little work done.

This Gene Morgan, being a Texan, is a great talker, and almost every story he tells is a bald-faced lie, until you check on it and find it to be truth absolute and undefiled.

He started right off by telling me about the baby-sitter cows. He knows an American who has a huge cattle ranch south of La Linda. "I have seen this with my own eyes," said Morgan, "so kindly omit your usual shrugging and eye-rolling and other gestures of disbelief and disgust. A herd of cows will start moving out early in the morning, heading for the good pasturage and leaving their calves behind. These calves would be subject to attack from all manner of wild beasts if they were left unguarded, so one cow stays with them and baby-sits. The entire herd seems to have a clear comprehension of this procedure, and at midday a relief sitter returns to the home pasture and takes over, so that the morning sitter can go out and get in on the gourmet grazing. By the way," Morgan concluded, "*these* baby-sitters almost never complain about not having television."

I shrugged and rolled my eyes heavenward and committed other gestures of disbelief and disgust. He insisted that we fly down to the ranch the next morning in one of his chartered Cessnas. "Ah'll show you, you smart-ellick Yankee," he said. I agreed, readily, but that evening a call came from my son who lived then in Lake Jackson, about five hundred miles to the east. He wanted me to come over for a visit so I took one of Morgan's planes and flew east, postponing the visit to the moocow baby-sitters.*

Anywhere that I travel I have to, out of strong habit, do some kind of research, and the pickin's were rather slim in the town of Lake Jackson, which is a small, neat community adjacent to Freeport at the mouth of the Brazos. So I interested myself in the town's street names. It looked as if every street in Lake Jackson was named for a tree, a shrub, or a flower: Chestnut, Mulberry, Carnation, Daffodil, Nasturtium, Cypress, Lantana, Trumpet Vine, Pecan, Primrose, Magnolia, Poinsettia, Mesquite, Chinaberry, Persimmon, and quite a few more. Then I discovered that there had been a rebellion, a revolt against this general pattern. I located a street called This Way and another, nearby, named That Way. Then I came upon North Blunk Road and South Blunk Road, and I went to the library to determine if there was such a thing as a blunk tree. There was not. Blunk was the name of a family who presumably didn't want their street named Horsechestnut, Sweetgum, or Pussy Willow.

During this splendid job of research I met the Bill Billingsleys, who run the local weekly newspaper. They fur-

---

* Later on Morgan bugged me so severely that I took oath that I would never go look at those cows. He sent me a bulletin published by Sul Ross College in which it was stated flatly and without equivocation that Texas cows "out of necessity originated the baby-sitting plan." The bulletin described the whole procedure, much as Morgan had described it. If there is anything I dislike it is a wrong person who somehow manages to be right.

nished me with some fine stories. They said that the former Kathy Grant, now Mrs. Bing Crosby, grew up in nearby West Columbia. There is a man in that town whose life revolves around a single incident, whose imperishable fame rests upon a single negative fact. West Columbia people point him out to visitors and say, "Once he asked Kathy Grant for a date and she turned him down." It is reported that he has ordered those words carved on his tombstone.

Mrs. Billingsley is a Callan from Menard County, up near San Angelo. The Callans have been an exciting and colorful family for long years, operating a cattle ranch of considerable dimension. They have made history. One Callan is celebrated as the very first man in West Texas to drive his automobile into a stump that was growing in the middle of the road, and getting thrown through the windshield in the process. The very first person to do it! In West Texas! Another Callan, Uncle Jim, was the one who killed a close relative of the notorious gunslinger, John Wesley Hardin. Uncle Jim killed the man because he had left a pasture gate open—a thing you didn't do even if your name was Hardin.

I decided that I ought to go up to Menard and visit some Callans. But another project came into my mind. I also wanted to journey to Austin and try to locate some of John Henry Faulk's friends and relatives. Mr. Faulk's tales of Texas people are never anything less than superb. He speaks of "my Aunt Mae Mae." He says, "Her Mama liked the name of Mae so much she give it to 'er twice." And I remembered his story of a country family with fourteen children and sixteen dogs. When the fifteenth child was born they went to the Old Man, as was their custom, and asked him what they should name the baby. He studied the matter for a bit and then said, "Ah just cain't think of one—we've used up all th' names on th' dawgs." On another occasion one of the boys fell out of an apple tree and broke his leg. When the Old Man was told about it he gave it some weighty consideration and then spoke philosophically: "It coulda been wuss—he coulda lit on one of th' dawgs."

It was a tough decision for me to make, as between John Henry Faulk's people and the Callans of Menard. While I was debating it in my mind, a call came from Gene Morgan urging me to come back to La Linda and eat some goat at a barbecue. I arranged to fly westward in a Cessna belonging to the Del Rio Flying Service and piloted by Herschel Moore. Herschel, a smallish, bald man, told me that the Robertson family, who ran the charter service, wanted me to set down at Del Rio and drink some coffee with them. We landed at their airport and they were waiting. The founding father, Bob Robertson, is a Texan of almost classical stamp, clad in a dark business suit, a cream-colored Stetson, and western boots; Hollywood could have cast him as owner of the biggest spread in the hull dern valley.

During our *kaffeeklatsch,* a Texas ceremonial more sacred than Men's Bible Class, Mr. Robertson happened to mention that he was from Menard County. "Well I be dogged," I said. "Does the name Callan mean anything to you?" He regarded me quizzically for a full twenty seconds and then he answered.

"Does the name *Callan* mean anything to me? Hah! Let me tell you a story. When I was a little boy I had been out visiting some kinfolks and I had to walk home. A long way. I came to this ranch and decided to go through it, a shortcut. I opened a wooden gate with the word *Callan* stenciled on it in big letters. Then I closed it and the word *Callan* was stenciled on the other side. A little farther along and I opened another gate with the word *Callan* on it, front and back. Then another one. Before I got to the far side of that ranch I had opened *one hundred and sixteen* gates with the word *Callan* on them. And you ask me if the word *Callan* means anything to me!"

The goat meat at La Linda was good.

NINE

A rasping twang was heard now in the vast prairie land. It was the voice of a character named Sam Huddleston, another columnist with Dallas as his base of iniquitous operation. This Huddleston said of my chili recipe that "a man could get more flavor from a set of stewed piano keys." He gave out that I knew less about a good bowl of chili than a pregnant sow knows about Neiman-Marcus.

"This dude," said Senor Huddleston, "ought to have his head candled." He charged that I was "one of them Yankees that've been spoiling up our womenfolks with washing machines and electric smoothin' irons."

I reckoned this Huddleston to be a common scold. I chose to ignore his tirade and went fishin'—a Cloralex expedition on the Rio Grande, organized by Gene Morgan at La Linda. There were four of us: Tom Leary, a native of the Big Bend country, owner of a cattle ranch between La Linda and Marathon, and proprietor of a drugstore in Marathon; Henhouse Hailey, a retired cattle rancher, a garrulous man in his early seventies; Gene Morgan himself, and me. Henhouse Hailey was called Henhouse because in his ranching days he spent more time feeling under hens for eggs than he spent with his cattle problems.

We assembled at the river's edge where a fourteen-foot

aluminum boat was waiting and where a couple of Mexicans had piled up two dozen green plastic bottles, labeled "Cloralex" which seems to be the name of a Mexican bleach. Each bottle had been stoppered and a nine-inch line fastened to the handle, with a small lead weight and a hook. The hooks had already been baited with chunklets of beef liver.

I remarked that when I was a kid we were accustomed to spitting on the bait, to make certain of a good catch.

"That's for worms," said Morgan. "Don't spit on this beef liver. Go on back and pollute your New York waters, but don't expectorate in our beautiful Rio Grande." I glanced at the water and thought of the classic description—too thick to drink and too thin to plow—and I thought too of my New York waters, the Hudson River, which has achieved the saturation point in pollution, being now but a mere nine per cent water.

The green bottles were turned loose in the river by the Mexicans. After all of them had been launched, we took our leisurely time arranging things in the boat—box lunches, thermos bottles of coffee, iced beer, a couple of cameras, binoculars. Then we shoved off in pursuit of the bobbing green bottles, which were all now out of sight.

Morgan began a story before we were ten feet from the shore.

"Shame you didn't get down this way for the funeral of Old Man Tatum's shotgun," he said. "Old Man Tatum lived in a shack near the river quite a piece below us, and his shack burnt down and his shotgun with it. He gethered up the remains and made a little coffin for them and got a few of his friends to go out one evening to a country graveyard. They didn't say any prayers but Old Man Tatum delivered a sort of farewell sermon."

Our boat was now approaching a canyon whose walls appeared to be half a mile high, but Morgan had been over this water many times and paid small heed to the scenic wonders. "There at the graveside," he went on, "Old Man Tatum took off his hat and he says, 'This is a sad day fer me, buryin' Ole Number Eight. It was down on Mistuh Gofoth's sandbar that it happened. Them geese come in to sand up. . . .'" Gene interrupted himself to explain that when geese sand up, they are getting grit into their crops to grind their food. "So Old Tatum says, 'Them geese was in perfect formation. I never had a chancet fer another shot like that before er sence. I lined 'em up and, blooooooey! Eight geese with one shot! Lord-a-mercy! If that ain't a world's record, then I don't know how to shoot geese. And if airy a shotgun desarved a public funeral, this one does. Good-bye, Ole Number Eight. Have youseff a long rest.'"

I enjoyed the tale but my mind was on catfish. This was the first real fishing I had undertaken since boyhood—if this could be called real fishing. When I was about twelve years old I used to fish with my father in the waters around the town of Defiance, Ohio, where the Auglaise and Maumee rivers conflue. Pop favored cane poles and night crawlers and my equipment was the same, with the addition of a cork out of a sorghum molasses jug. Pop scorned bobbers of any kind and eventually converted me away from them. "A carp," he said, "won't go near a bobber 'les he's starvin' to death—he thinks it's some kinda battleship."

In those far-gone days I realized that fishermen practice a religion of their own or, rather, each individual fisherman embraces a code of orthodox beliefs fully as occult and complex as Spin-off Shintoism. Articles in the various creeds proclaim that fish will never bite during a thunderstorm and remain scared, hugging bottom, for two or three days after such a storm; that when the cows are lying down in the pastures, the bass are hitting; that if an east wind is blowing, pack up your tackle and go home; that trout find hidey-holes on the bottom if there are any female wimmin around. There is a great body of such scientific knowledge, but somehow the True Faith failed to snatch me and after my family left Ohio I never fished again.

When we were entering the canyon I asked Gene Morgan to tell me something about the fish we were pursuing, and Henhouse Hailey spoke up: "It ain't a good idee," he said, "to ever talk about catfish when you are out to get catfish. They won't get in a country moll uh your hooks you start talkin' about 'em."

I pointed out that the bottles were probably a mile (moll) out in front of us by now, and the catfish couldn't hear us gossiping about them, and then Morgan said that almost the only fish ever taken from the Rio Grande, at least in this area, are blue cat, channel cat, and mud cat. "Some of the mud cat run as high as ninety pound," he said, "and they are . . ."

"Speakin' of raddlesnakes," spoke up Henhouse Hailey, "you oughta see the ones we got back home. Once a year we have a raddlesnake roundup, everbody with forked sticks and warr nooses and gunny sacks, ketch 'em by the hunderds. Up home we *know* raddlesnakes. A full-growed one ain't a particle afraid of nobody. It sickens me to hear all these experts sayin' that a raddlesnake won't bother you long as you don't bother him. Bull roar! Don't ever bleeve it! He'll come at you because he hates you and he knows he can lick you. But he's a gennelman, clean through. He walks right up to you and says, 'Ah'll fight you no holts barred, whether you wanna fight er not, so flang up yer dukes.' No, sirreee. A raddlesnake don't sneak around and ambush people. He fights fair and he kills honest."

Our shiny craft was now in the canyon where the stream narrowed, roughing up the water, but we weathered the tossing about we got and I, in fact, rather enjoyed it. Our journey was to cover fifteen moll of river and take about three hours. When we came out of the canyon into scrubby, dusty-looking flat land again, Gene Morgan launched into a story about a raffle he had recently organized among the Mexicans of La Linda. Gene had a bottle of 25-year-old scotch and decided to raise some money for charity with it. He consulted with a couple of Mexican associates and learned that raffles in their land are somewhat different from those in Estados Unidos. In the first place, said Morgan, a Mexican prizes a bottle of genuine scotch above almost all other possessions. With him it is a status symbol, and stands prominently on a shelf or table in his living room, and when the whisky is all gone he still keeps it there, filled with colored water. So the interest in the raffle was intense, and a one-day fiesta was declared, for it takes a full day to conduct a Mexican raffle. More than a hundred chances were sold at a dollar apiece and as soon as the fiesta got started, two men stood by the box and at a signal from Morgan, drew out a name. Santanna Chavez.

"I got up to congratulate Santanna," Morgan said, "and right at this point I learned that a Mexican raffle runs backwards. The first name chosen is not the winner. He is eliminated, and so is the second, and third, and so on down to the point where a single name remains in the box. He wins the whisky. The drawing started early in the morning and continued intermittently to the final moments of the party late that night. You can imagine how the suspense built up all during the day. One of the most exciting blow-outs I've ever attended in Mexico."

The river twisted and turned, and narrowed and widened, and the scenic wonders continued awesome, alternating between grandeur and desiccated bleakness. My god when I get to writing about scenery I *write* it. There was no sign of life anywhere outside the boat, and there was no sign of any green bottles.

Tom Leary now spoke up: "Along this stretch of the river, I think this is where the Apaches used to snatch ducks. They'd locate a flight settled on the water. Then they'd hide

85

in the bushes and begin releasing big gourds. These gourds would float along, into the flock, and for some reason the ducks didn't seem to be afraid of the invaders. So after a while when the birds had become accustomed to the gourds, those Apaches would put big gourds over their heads, with eyeholes cut in them, and creep into the water, crouching so only the gourds would show. They'd move into the flight of ducks and the way they took them was to reach up from below, take hold of their legs, and jerk them under water, where they stuffed them in bags held below the surface."

By this time it seemed clear to me that the minds of my companions were not on fishing, to the exclusion of all other subjects. I felt that I had to get into the act, so I told General Ed Sebree's story of the time Horse Wagner and Willie Biggerstaff went coon-huntin' in the land of my nativity, Little Egypt. They were deep in the woods, in proven coon country, when they noted a scurrying in the bushes and caught a glimpse of an animal ducking into a large hollow log. Willie Biggerstaff got down on his knees and tried to grab the critter, but couldn't reach him, so he bent lower and poked his face up to the opening. Zwisssssh! It was not a coon. It was a polecat, and Willie got the charge full in his eyes. Woods people know that skunk juice can blind a man permanently. Willie rolled over groaning, and Horse Wagner went into action. Horse had a chaw in his cheek, and he knew that tobacco juice is a specific remedy for skunk juice in the eyes. Carefully he deposited some tobacco juice in Willie's eyes. Willie heaved a deep sigh of relief and then murmured, as though in ecstasy, "Godamighty, Hoss, do that ag'in!"

Gene Morgan now resumed his discourse on the nature of the catfish, which is considered a delicacy on both sides of the Tex–Mex border. "There's no prejudice against him," said the big Texan, "the way there is in certain other parts of the country, especially among you knothead Yankees.

Way I figure, by the time we get to Maravillas we'll have enough catfish for a combination fish fry and fiesta for the whole village of La Linda."

"But where," I asked, "are the catfish at? Wharr did them ole green bottles go to?"

Henhouse Hailey came to life again. He told a long and involved story about a couple of fishermen back in North Carolina, a man named Charlie Ross and another man named Jack Starrett, and by the time the tale was completed we were coming out of Heath Canyon. Tom Leary spotted a green bottle moving erratically near the Texas shore and Morgan saw one farther along. Out came the oars and soon we had our first catfish, one about three feet long, the other a foot shorter. I had been wondering how we would ever catch up to those bottles, considering the fact that they floated at the same speed as our boat. Morgan explained that catfish are usually mule-stubborn and hate to ever swim downstream, so as soon as they took hold of the bait, they'd begin struggling uphill, so to speak, or at least drag the green bottle over to still water near the shore. I was looking at the bigger of the cats we had caught and concluding that this *had* to be the ugliest, meanest-looking critter on earth; he somehow made me think of Damon Runyon, a friendly man who somehow had the misfortune to look catfish-mean, and then seen from another angle, our catfish resembled a certain book reviewer back East. Henhouse Hailey interrupted my ruminations.

"Ah'm a man," he said, "likes to make mah own buttuh. Ah skin the cream offa the milk and put it in a quawt jar till it's a couple inches from the top, and screw on the lid, and start shakin' it. Shake it thirty minutes or a hour. Shake it this-away, shake it thataway, down, up, crossways, waggle it aroun', keep on shakin'. Ah don't like to waste time by just standin' still and shakin' a jar, so Ah try to find somethin' else to do, and maybe walk aroun' mah yod and look at thangs. So folks come drivin' past and I can almost heah them sayin', 'Lookit ole Henhouse, gone plumb in-sane, walkin' aroun' his yod shakin' a quawt jar.' Ah pay 'em no mind. Went to San Tone once, went in a place called Frisky A Go Go, godderndest dancin' in there, like wile Indinns. Thought maybe Ah'd invent a new modrun dance, call it the Buttuh Jar Shake. Never got aroun' to it."

Adrift again, I spoke of a piece I'd seen in the New York *Times* about a boy fishing for trout in a Wyoming lake, using small-size marshmallows for bait and hauling in the gleaming beauties on a day when the weisenheimers were getting nothing with their fly rods. Morgan said that the Mexicans are dedicated to beef liver but when they don't have it they use a laundry soap called Mariposa (butterfly) and do real well with it.

Henhouse asked me if I had ever heard tell of a Texan named Brit Bailey, and I said I hadn't. "One uh the nobel-est Texans ever lived," he said. "Had hisself buried standin' up straight in the grave, rifle over his shoulder, jug uh whisky at his feet, said by god he was a Texan and even when he was dead he wasn't gonna look up to any man alive."

We entered Horse Canyon and the river narrowed and we were soon shooting the rapids. Just as we emerged from the canyon with a rush, the boat hit a rock, bounced back, went on past the rock and hit a bigger rock, and over we went. A Mexican goat-herder was on the south bank and witnessed our disaster and doubled up with laughter. Then he waded out and helped us get the boat ashore. Everything else was gone—food, cameras, binoculars, catfish. Morgan was furious at the goat-herder, and demanded to know what he found so funny about the accident, and the Mexican told him in Spanish that when we hit the first rock all he could see was four butts sticking straight up in the air. Butts, apparently, are as funny in Mexico as they are elsewhere. We took off our clothes and wrung them out, and then put them back on, and climbed into our dented boat to proceed down-river to Maravillas where the pickup truck was waiting to haul us back home. The delay had been a long one, and we saw no more green bottles.

And so, after a while, we arrived at Maravillas Creek, a spot known to old-timers as "the fartherest away from no-where of any place on earth." We saw smoke on the Mexican shore, and the pickup, and the glint of the sun on green bottles. It turned out that a dozen or so Mexican wetbacks, preparing to cross the river and proceed up the dry bed of the creek to find work, spotted the green bottles in the river. The wetbacks waded in and captured eight or ten nice catfish. With the assistance of our Mexican truck driver, they built a fire, got out their crude utensils and their lard, and prepared a riverside fish fry. They were just finishing their feast when we arrived. We were still wet, and hungry, but we'd have to wait for provender until we got back to La Linda.

And so, after a lovely steak supper, we were sitting on the veranda at the ranch house and Morgan said, "I'm sorry about it, but it couldn't be hepped. Worse dern fishin' trip I was ever on. I apologize to you, you Yankee Joner."

I had been busy scribbling in my notebook. "Gene," I said, "no apologies necessary. It was a marvelous expedition. If we'd have gone fifty miles instead of fifteen, I'd have got me a whole book. Fishin'," I concluded, "is a whole lot more than just fishin'."

TEN

I had sent no word to Dallas accepting Wick Fowler's challenge, yet when I returned to New York again I learned that the Texas people were going ahead arrogantly and planning the contest for this town named Terlingua on the 21st of October. Rules were being drawn up and travel arrangements organized. No one asked me a thing. There had been no formal approach to me and by god I'm a man who goes in for formality. My agent, Harold Matson, informed me that he had heard about the Fowler challenge only through reading about it in a newspaper. The Texans were proceeding blithely and childishly without even consulting one of the two principals involved.

I had work to do on a book and several magazine articles about Texas to get written; yet, even if I had had plenty of time on my hands, I would have resisted this high-handed procedure. I bode my time until someone in Dallas called and reported, excitedly, that "everything's all set and we'll expect you here in Dallas a few days ahead of time."

"You," I replied, "can go fart up a flagpole. If you expect me in Dallas you are insane. I am not coming to Dallas and I am not coming out to that Terllydingle. You guys got a helluva nerve." I hung up.

The high command of the Chili Appreciation Society

began flopping around in old-fashioned country-style fits. They held emergency meetings. They had their Big Bend fiesta all set up, planes chartered, officials appointed, publicity campaign in full swing, and now this Yankee Smith was balking. They schemed and connived, coming up with all sorts of stratagems through which they might pressure me into accepting the challenge. They could not understand that I work for nobody but myself, that I have no boss, belong to no political party or lodge, adhere to no church, that I am as independent as eight javelinas on ice, and that I consider any and all types of pressure, including especially that highly respected institution the American congressional lobby, to be evil and crooked and criminal. I said I wasn't coming, and that they couldn't even shame me into coming.

It came to my attention that X. Tolbert had been in communication with his paper's Washington correspondent, Karen Klinefelter (I told you those Dallas people do *every-thing* on a large and flamboyant scale). Miss Klinefelter, functioning on the theory that the chili cook-off was a foreordained fact, approached Congressman J. J. Pickle of Austin and Mr. Pickle got in touch with Miss Betty Furness, special assistant to President Johnson for Consumer Affairs. The pressure was on for a public statement on the subject of chili by Miss Furness. She issued one. She said that she was aware of the fact that "the chili problem certainly supersedes all others. It has aroused violent passions in the hearts of men and has caused a severe drain on our national economy as the public becomes distracted from drinking coffee and eating steak." Miss Furness added that she was "pleased to learn that this matter will be settled for all time to come."

I still had not accepted the challenge.

In one Gargantuan, shrill and drawly chorus, the State of Texas arose on its hind legs and cried out in my direction: "Chicken!" I stood my ground, and then one afternoon I

91

happened again on the letter from Wayne Sargent describing the innate spinelessness of Texas husbands; at that same moment *Holiday* Magazine called and said they'd pay my expenses and undertake to buy another article from me if I'd go to Terlingua. This put a slightly different color on the sagebrush. I was turning the thing over in my mind, and thinking that, in cold actuality, I *do* make a better pot of chili than anything Wick Fowler slings together, when another desperate call came from one of the Dallas promoters. He *begged* me to come. He all but offered me oil money in large sums if I would come. He said that Dave Chasen from Beverly Hills was coming, and bringing Elizabeth Taylor in a special plane. He said that Chasen would have to be thrown into the breach as a sub for me if I failed to come; he said two or three of the astronauts had accepted invitations, and the Governor would probably be there, and maybe even the President. I capitulated.

The next thing I heard was that X. Tolbert had approached two other prominent characters with invitations—Phyllis Diller and Walter Jetton. Miss Diller, it was reported, turned him down in a statement to the California press complaining that Tolbert had said her hair-do and her personality would blend nicely with the harsh, desiccated, rancid scenery around Terlingua. Walter Jetton, who was barbecuer-in-waiting to the President and somewhat celebrated in his own right as a chili cook, was asked to attend and do some sideline cooking for the crowds; he declined on the grounds of illness (he died several months later) but said he would send some people who worked for his catering service.

A man named Ben Isadore Waldman, who claims that he was only temporarily absent from Texas when he was born, came forward with the statement that chili was invented by the Jews. This bit of interesting history was picked up by Maury Maverick, Jr., in a long article he undertook for the San Antonio *Express-News*. Mr. Maverick, after discussing plans for the Terlingua Confrontation, made some slighting remarks about me, his former buddy, and then embarked upon a rather depraved and perverted history of chili.

A few fragments from the writings of Maverick:

Consider the words of Isaiah of the Old Testament. He is the wise man often quoted by the distinguished rancher from the Pedernales River ("Come let us reason together") when things are not going so good. "For the plowman doth scatter the cumin," wrote this major prophet, Isaiah, that is, not Lyndon.

References to the tithing of grain in Deuteronomy 14 and Leviticus 27 are interpreted by the Mishna, the written codification of the Judaic oral law, to include cumin. In any event the Jews had a hand in the beginning of chili for they told the Moors about cumin, who told the Canary Islanders, who brought the herb to San Antonio. Thank goodness other cultures picked it up, else all we might have had today would be *chili con matzo balls.*

Through the metamorphosis that has come to be modern chili, the Jews gave Texas Isaiah, the Mexicans came through with the chefs of Montezuma, the Anglo's contribution is Wick Fowler. But the story does not stop there; it dare not for how could the Teutonic gift of William Gebhardt to this great dish be ignored?

Prior to Gebhardt, the processing of chile peppers was a tedious process. The stem and seed would be removed, and pulp forced through a sieve to get the necessary paste. But around 1890, Gebhardt successfully came up with the idea of grinding several of the necessary herbs into one delicious powder which, in those early days, he called "Tampico Dust. . . ."

There is not much more to be said except to again point out the threat presented by H. Allen Smith to Texas in general, and to San Antonio in particular. Let us forget our differences as the moment of the great chili duel approaches. Let the AFL–CIO and the Chamber of Commerce be one army. Let the doves and the hawks be one bird. No longer can we be Republican or Democrat.

The hour of high noon is but days away. If Smith doesn't chicken out at the last minute, we must rally to the defender of our honor, old 2-Alarm Wick Fowler. Indeed, a failure on the part of any of us chili-heads to attend this great event is enough to remind one of the words of King Henry IV of France: "Hang yourself, brave Crillon, we have conquered at Argues, and you were not there."

As Colonel Travis took his sword and drew the famous line at the Alamo, I, with my chili spoon, draw a line across which all men and women of courage must surely step with heads held high.

Gentle readers, patriots, Texas chili-heads everywhere—will you be at Terlingua?

Throughout this long and garbled disquisition Maury Maverick abused me wherever possible. He called me "the Mount Kisco tiger" and said that I was a mad genius. When it came to describing my work, he mentioned several of my books and weakened and said they were "all literary gems ranking alongside Edward Gibbon's *Decline and Fall of the Roman Empire*. He had to say that. He could not fly in the face of overwhelming public opinion.

Maverick rather enjoyed the notion of his idiotic statement that the Jews invented chili, or had a hand in inventing it, and in a subsequent communication to X. Tolbert he went over that ground again, concluding: "Everyone knows I am an Episcopalian and therefore I am automatically telling the truth."

I had to answer this former friend, this Benedict Arnold of La Villita on the banks of the San Antonio River. I did so in these words; addressed to the editor of the San Antonio *Express-News:*

Martin Mayer, a New York gentleman, recently published a book called *The Lawyers.* Mr. Mayer contends that he loves lawyers and that his book is a warm and friendly salute to the profession, yet he manages somehow to suggest that if you scratch an attorney you will uncover rattlesnake meat. I am suggesting that Mr. Mayer go back to press with a new edition of his book, containing an added chapter titled, "Look Out for Perfidy, Also." That chapter will be about Maury Maverick, Jr.

Last week's feuilleton, which Mr. Maverick wrote for the *Express-News* in collaboration with his wife, his law partners, his chiropodist, and his office boy, is a tissue of organic fertilizer. He has turned on me, a friend. And he has sinfully accepted appointment as the "neutral" judge of the Great Chili Cook-Off at Terlingua. Neutral my hind foot! Mr. Maverick is a Texan.

My war is a war with 209 male (not masculine) citizens of Dallas, and one hen-headed citizen of Austin named Wick Fowler. A fowler is a despoiler of little birds. A wick is a hunk of rag stuck in a container of oil. It burns with a flickering, smelly flame. This Wick Fowler, I believe, will burn with the searing flame of ignominy at Terlingua on March 21st at high noon.

High noon! A fitting hour for treachery! Gary Cooper had no one but Colby and Pearce and the blackhearted Miller brothers to vanquish in his high noon encounter. I have 209 childish lardheads and a houseboat jockey, not to mention a perfidious lawyer.

I Shall Overcome.

In fact I have them all on the run. This last week I got word from Austin that Wick Fowler and his Dallas henchmen have gone into panic. Wick has lost his cool. The truth has come upon him that a time-tested proverb we have in

New York is correct. We say: "You cannot get a decent piece of meat in Texas."

Wick Fowler and his Dallas goon squad have been holding secret gatherings, testing meat with their teeth, trying to chomp through all available cuts of Texas beef. At length the realization reached them that Wick cannot beat me.

Crying and groaning in agonized tones, these villains finally arrived at a conclusion. They would have to locate something other than Texas beef to use in Fowler's Bowl-of-Mud. So they drug Fowler, that smelly wick, into an underground laboratory at the University of Texas and set him to working around the clock, seeking a substitute for the chopped motorman's glove he has been accustomed to using.

A chemistry professor happened by and saw their dilemma and told them to beg me for a small amount of my miracle chemical, sassatate; the professor said that my sassatate would tenderize Texas beef so that a person with sound teeth would be able to tell it from a hame-strap. I refused to give them so much as an ounce of sassatate, and the professor advised them to throw in the towel. To Wick Fowler he said: "Take a coil of rope and wander into the woods. . . ."

Dallas people, I must confess, are inclined to be loud-mouthy and biggety. They tried to impress me by offering me a ride from their city to Terlingua in a chartered plane. I told them I would cook against them, but I would not mix with them socially. Their magnificent offer did not dampen my underthings. Twenty-odd years ago before any of those pepper-bellied blowhards had clumb trembling and slavering in terror into his first flying machine, I had grown weary of driving in Georgia and at Augusta chartered a plane to fly both me and my automobile back to New York.

Nor could they impress me by loudly announcing that I was going to have the high privilege of supping with both Toots Shor and Bob Considine. Those two slobs! That I, the pal of princes, the confidant of gaekwars, the crony of presidential advisors, the man who drove Elizabeth into the arms of Richard, that *I* should be impressed by scum! . . .

I warn Maury Maverick. He'd better not push me too far. I'm liable to say something harsh about the Alamo.

Texans actually have no pride. The *Express-News* printed my answer to Maverick, including that temperate and reasonable criticism of Texas beef. And Wick Fowler reacted to it in this wise:

"Terlingua, as you may know, is not a metropolis, nor can it boast of attractions such as the HemisFair. In fact the city is too small to have a village idiot. Residents have to take turns. We plan to confer upon Smith a citation as an Honorary Idiot of Terlingua."

Clippings were flooding in from every quarter of Texas. It seemed to me that half the journalists of the State were writing little essays and cruddy editorials on the subject of chili and the coming Confrontation; and they were calling me names, including the foulest they could think of—"a New York book author." To use Bob Hope's ancient phrase, it was obvious that every one of these journalists, at college, majored in Nasty.

Carroll Abbott of Kerrville, a man long prominent in both Texas journalism and Texas politics, communicated with me on behalf of one of his publications, a magazine devoted to the veneration of the Texas Longhorn, and called by that name. Texans are so reverent toward this almost extinct animal that they insist upon his name being capitalized and the Texas Historical Lobby has pressured the dictionary people with such persistence and power that the dictionaries do capitalize it. Scandalous.

Mr. Abbott advised me that he was preparing an article proving that chili originated in longhorn country, and he offered me his reasoning. He wanted some comment from me, and I presented him with the following:

With gratification bordering on hysteria I now learn that the *Texas Longhorn* has proclaimed and decreed that chili came into existence because of the Texas longhorn. The reference is to the critter, not the publication. Something to do with tough meat. On the critter, not the magazine. What in God's name am I saying? This thing begins to sound daffy before I can even get it well started. What this bovinistic magazine is trying to say is the equivalent of *my* trying to say that heel-meat off the hooves of Wick Fowler started up chili.

Set a man to ruminating about the beginnings of chili and you'll soon have a man babbling nonsense, especially if he's a full-blooded Texan. In recent months I have heard it stated with zest and authority that chili came into being because it was necessary to get rid of certain tough and stringy meats, such as undercoating of armadillo, the thigh-parts of road-runners, javelina knuckles, and rump steak from the flare-out behinds of Brewster County antelope.

This sort of balderdash has been showing up regularly in learned journals, such as the one you are reading. It's enough to make a grown man spit up. To use Professor Parkinson's language, collars are getting hot under. Including mine. I even hear that Wick Fowler himself is working up a theory that chili originated among the Karankawa Indians of Padre Island, who were wont to eat one another dipped in hot sauce.

One thing is certain: Texas chili, in the recent past, has usually *looked* as if it had been made from the meat of elderly and rachitic longhorns—possibly from their tail-knots. But since my arrival on the scene Texans have found out just how much pure shimmering beauty can be bubbled into a bowl of red under a master's hand. Texans, at last, are learning to cook chili the way chili ought to be cooked. My way.

Still this kind of talk keeps up. Longhorn chowder indeed! My friends, please let us forego talk of cow-critter tail-knots and all sitch as that and just sit down and enjoy a good bowl of chili. I make this appeal to reason with the full knowledge that it will do no good. Next month some kook will come along with solid proof that chili originated because men had to get rid of their old rodeo saddles and Mexican wallets they got for Christmas.

There is no end to human folly. There is no hope for man.

ELEVEN

In San Antonio, Maury Maverick, Jr., began circulating reports that I planned on bringing tainted New York beef to Terlingua and he issued a public statement urging that federal meat inspectors lay for me at the Vicksburg bridge and clap me in irons. This San Antonio shyster's accusation made no sense, of course, unless he believed that I had cooked up a scheme to switch meat on Wick Fowler. I would never switch anything on Wick Fowler, most especially meat. That would be sheer madness on my part.

I had eaten of Texas meat aplenty, and Texas meat is the meat used by Fowler in his chili. I repeat, I do not know why it is that Texas butchers are unable to pass good meat across their counters. The usual alibi has it that Texas sends all its good beef to the East and retains the neck-stuff and other gristly remainders for its own people. Some non-Texans, resident in Lone Stardom, have told me that Texas butchers don't know how to age beef and on top of that, don't know how to cut meat properly. It seems a great mystery and a shame; yet I assure my readers that I cannot remember ever having a steak in Texas that I could exclaim over, a steak to compare even with those I broiled over charcoal a couple of times a week at my home in New York. The only explanation that will hold any water is this: the

Texas consumer just doesn't know any better. I have been to Texas homes many times when the host has broiled steaks in the yod, and then I have seen the Texans pitch in heartily and eat those steaks, crying out in ecstasy between bites, saying, "Man oh man, what goowuhd steaks! Whirred you buy 'em, Billy?" And I have been at those same tables, unable to bite through the leathery meat.

In reply to the Maverick charge of meat-switching, then, I issued a calm and dignified statement: "Maury Maverick has misplaced his marbles."

Meanwhile Tolbert the Terrible was sitting at his typewriter in Dallas day after day, grinding his teeth and giving off feeble prosody. He continually referred to Wick Fowler as "recognized champion" among the world's chili-makers, and to me as "Soupy" Smith. He inserted half-column cuts of Ben Turpin, Bull Montana, King Kong, and Phyllis Diller into the body of his column, identifying each one as "that ole H. A." or as "Soupy." He told about a cocktail party that was being planned for the evening of cook-off day and, being a great humanitarian, he began some old-woman worrying for chili-eating drunks. "There are," he wrote, "a lot of open mine shafts in Terlingua, once the cinnabar mining capital of this nation." (I love the man's scintillating prose style.)

"Guests, including Soupy Smith," he informed the people of Dallas, "will sleep in bedrolls at the headquarters of the Terlingua Ranch owned by David Witts and Carroll Shelby, the Los Angeles racing car driver and manufacturer of the deodorant, Pit Stop." I promptly notified Tom Tierney, the Dallas public relations man who had been installed as "matchmaker" for the cook-off, that X. Tolbert was not telling *me* how I was going to sleep, that I was a civilized man, and that I wouldn't sleep in a bedroll if Elizabeth Taylor and Angie Dickinson were rolled in it with me. Since then I have had second thoughts on the matter.

X. wrote that I was already, in advance, making public

101

apology for my chili. He had reference to my explanation about the bell pepper—an explanation that satisfied everyone else, for I am known far and wide as a man of integrity who would not commit a lie about bell peppers. "The truth seems to be," mused Tolbert, taking on the cast of gentle philosopher, "that Smith didn't know any more about chili or chili-making than a hog does about a buggy whip until a year or so ago when he discussed the subject with a real chili expert, Maury Maverick, Jr., of San Antonio." He referred to my sparkling *Holiday* essay as an "ignoramus article" and charged me with bad-mouthing my wife. At another point he called me "the aged challenger." Once, and only once, he quoted me *in* context and my butt was in a sling.

Along about this time Governor John Connally proclaimed Saturday, October 21, 1967, as "Chili Appreciation Day" which I thought was tilting it pretty heavy in the direction of the Dallas crowd.

Sam Huddleston the Smart Ellick writes a column for a sleazy rag called *Outdoor Times.* It is, you may be sure, published in Dallas. Members of its staff stay outdoors all the time, for obvious reasons. Mr. Huddleston was cracking on sail, if that is the correct expression. Here are some paragraphs from his mush *refrito:*

> If you get this Yankee Smith in a tight corner he will admit to being the Chili King of all America, including Waxahachie. What this critter calls real chili is a slurpy Mother Whistler type of vegetable stew thinner than diluted water. . . .
>
> As you can plainly see members of the Texas-based Chili Appreciation Society are bull-roaring mad and demand a

showdown. I have been doing some research in available chili encyclopedias and papers and I don't find H. Allen Smith's name mentioned. In fact he didn't even get a call plumb around the track. . . .

This Yankee carpetbagger who wears a stovepipe hat and handlebar moustache has a cunning look in the tail of his good eye and as to trickery he should be on a Special Mention list.

He is as smooth as baby food and will cut you down with surgical precision without even turning a cool hair. You surely do have to keep your big brown eyes on *this* one.

When Ol' H. A. comes to Texas, and he will be here as sure as the due date on a bank note, it wouldn't surprise me if he didn't slink into Terlingua with ample quantities of prime Texas bull meat and with plenty of Mr. Fowler's 2-Alarm Chili mix, plus Frank Tolbert's chili bible called "A Bowl of Red," which will show him how to make chili beans supreme. With a bed of live mesquite coals to simmer up the aforementioned vittlements, Ol' H. A. would have some formidable artillery. It is possible that he might even blow Wick Fowler off the chili throne with Mr. Fowler's own ammunition. Ol' H. A. is a fighter—make no mistake about it!

I was startled to note that Smart Ellick Huddleston suffers from a glimmering of North Carolina-type extrasensory perception. Back in New York I had a crate of chili mix shipped to me by Wick Fowler himself. I spent some time eying it. I was almost certain that the Texans would try to swindle me; I was convinced that the State sport in Texas is the con game and that the most popular hobby amongst Texans is larceny —sometimes called *business.* They would try to hornswoggle me fore and aft, they would try to steal the contest, for that is their immutable way of life. The thought occurred to me that I might take Wick Fowler's processed chili ingredients, transfer them to my own jugs and cruets, buy myself some gristly Texas meat, and beat those dirty bastards at their own game. If I undertook this mild bit of deception, I couldn't lose. If the decision of the judges gave me the championship, I would just smile and swagger a bit and keep my mouth shut. If the judgment went against me, I would simply step forward with affidavits proving that my ingredients were precisely the same as Fowler's ingredients. I would demonstrate the crummy dishonesty of the Dallas-bribed judges; I would demonstrate that Wick Fowler had won cooking against his own chili. But now this scrofulous roadrunner Sam Huddleston had blown my scheme sky-high. The Dallas dog-kickers are semiliterate and mildly moronic, but they own a certain animal cunning, like the Texas coyote. I couldn't take the chance.

This Huddleston Thing went on:

All the world knows we Texans have an inborn fear of any kind of overstatement or exaggeration concerning Texas or Texans, so I will carry on this fine tradition by being impartial and reporting only the true facts.

This here Yankee H. Allen Smith don't know nothin' about makin' chili. What he tries to saw off on the public for chili is a water-thin concoction of anemic vegetables which tastes like rescue mission soup. A whole tubful of this stuff wouldn't give a killdee enough energy to get off her nest. Men in Texas have been hung for less than what Ol' H. A. has done to the name of chili. All America knows that our own Wick Fowler is a curly coyote when it comes to making chili. From his first germ plasm he was preordained to wear the chili championship crown. Not since the days of antiquity has any hombre ever made a better cotton-pickin' bowl of chili than Old Wick, and if you don't believe it you just ask him. . . .

I don't figure Ol' H. A. would weigh in as a very talented chili-maker, but don't underplay his other talents. This dude is a cool stud and can see around corners and think on his feet. He has a well-honed brain and resorting to trickery surely won't lacerate his conscience. . . . I received a report that Ol' H. A. once stole an old-fashioned reading lamp off an upstate New York farmer's table and he did it so fast the farmer just kept on reading.

Simple Sam concluded his remarks with some advice to people who might be planning the trip to Terlingua. "If you don't have reservations," he said, "you can use a Laredo bed. A Laredo bed is where you use your back for a mattress and cover up with your stomach."

In San Antonio a character named Sam Woolford began creepy-crawling into the act. Woolford composes a column for the San Antonio *Light,* a newspaper which farms out book review assignments to needy children. Woolford assaulted me initially by criticizing the town where I lived. Each time he referred to Mount Kisco he emphasized the *Mount* and specified that its elevation was 165 feet—500 feet lower than the Southern Pacific depot in San Antonio.

This Woolford proved to be a recidivous snot. He pecked away at me and my chili like a sick roadrunner working over a lizard. He suggested that anyone having an interest in tasting my chili should be prepared to use a soda straw—a notion plagiarized right out of my original *Holiday* article. In running through my recipe he made childish comments like this: " 'Then add your beans.' Who else's beans are we supposed to add, you damn Yankee?" Woolford worked himself into such a snit that he began low-rating Terlingua.

"In its glorious heydey (the man can't even spell) of quicksilver mining," he wrote clumsily, "I have eaten there, slept there, sweated there, and been ordered off the premises. And I have never been able to understand why I went there in the first place." He said that forty years ago he, wise Woolford, had described Terlingua as "the land God forgot, where the Devil built a playground." He demanded to know why a chili-making contest should be held "in this desolate land where Spanish goat meat and Rio Grande catfish were all the folks had to eat anyway."

Woolford expressed satisfaction that J. Frank Dobie had not lived to witness what I was doing to chili. This from a man who remains idiotically loyal to a town that, by conservative estimate, has 58,815 different barbecue sauces—one for each and every resident.

Woolford next sets himself up as a scholarly person and perching his pince-nez on the end of his ocotillo nose, undertakes to trace the history of chili. He strikes out immediately. He doesn't even seem able to grasp the fact that there is a difference between chili and chile—between the bowl of red and the hot pepper.

Finally, Somnolent Sam suggests a method of disposing of my brand of chili as follows:

> Select eight large prickly-pear leaves, well cured in the sun. Do not bother to remove the thorns. Arrange each artistically on a cedar shake. Over a slow fire baste cactus leaves with residue of Smith's "ambrosia." Do not rush. Baste frequently, if not oftener. The idea is to get the rest of his chili imbedded into the lacelike pithy structure of the nopal leaf. As the sun slowly sinks in the West, carefully stack the now tender cactus leaves and their piquant sauce in a neat pile near a prairie-dog colony; hose off the shingles, stack them in a safe place. They are liable to start a fire.
>
> In time, if properly placed in your house, these shingles will deter scorpions, sowbugs, sugar ants, moths, cockroaches, and even mosquitoes. It might even be possible that they would discourage rattlesnakes.

That's enough from Brother Woolford and his shingles. I have not tried his recipe for cedar shakes impregnated with my chili. I may give it a whirl in the event I find myself some day planning a visit to San Antonio. If it should turn out that the chili imparts fiery puissance to the shingle, and with the full knowledge that a cedar shake has a rough surface and sharp and rugged edges, I know precisely where I would like to shove one or two, in tandem.

A letter came from Aileen Benninghoff who lives in Brecksville, Ohio, south of Cleveland. Following the appearance of the Pragmatic Sanction in *Holiday* Mrs. Benninghoff, a book reviewer and lecturer with a wide following and an old friend of mine, began throwing chili parties right and left, using my recipe with major success. She said it was necessary for her to have copies of my recipe Xeroxed in quantity, because each lady who took on a bowl of my chili—if her alimentary canal could stand it—demanded the formula.

"Cumin is new to me," Mrs. Benninghoff said. "I found it in the Westfield Drug Store. The clerk said she had seen mounds of it in the shops in Morocco. I am now cumin-happy. Add a dash to eggs, scrambled or deviled. Meat loaf, too, and Bill tastes his coffee each morning with apprehension. Thanks a lot for a conversation-piece meal."

(Now another digression, with a very mild cookery angle.)

Not long ago this same Aileen Benninghoff sent me a newspaper clipping about the fireplace in her home at Brecksville. The principal material used in constructing the fireplace is pink sandstone, and set into the facing are rocks which the Benninghoffs have collected as mementos of their extensive travels.

Each of these rocks is like rosemary, for remembrance, and reminds the Benninghoffs of the pleasures they've had in faraway places. There are agates from the Yukon and from Montana; rose quartz hacked off a Lover's Leap in South Dakota; a fragment of granite from Mount Rushmore and a stone from a mountain to the south of Rushmore where Korczak Ziolkowski is unceasingly and incessantly carving his colossal statue of the great Sioux chieftain, Crazy Horse. (Ziolkowski will be entering these pages again shortly.)

The Benninghoff fireplace serves as more of a conversation piece than my chili, but not quite as adequately as the fireplace in the home of Lowell Thomas, at Pawling, New York. Mr. Thomas, his friends have told me, has a fireplace made entirely of rocks he has fetched from travels all over the world. Name any remote corner of the globe and Mr. Thomas has been there, and put a local rock in his pocket. It is said that he can stand by that fireplace and point, and talk two hours about the localities where he acquired each stone. This is nice, to be sure, but too much of it would be a bit like hauling out the family album, or showing home movies of the children when they were learning to walk. I doubt that Mr. Thomas does this fireplace lecture very often, for he is a man with an astringent attitude toward the steady foolishness of his fellow creatures.

It must be that there are other fireplaces around the nation belonging to people who have gathered special rocks in their travels. I made preparations, a couple of years ago, to build one of my own and I speak of it here because my projected fireplace was for cooking.

My home, in the outer suburbs of New York City, was served by the New York Central. Between my house and the city, stretched alongside the Central tracks, are vast acres devoted to cemeteries. They seem to flow together into one immense graveyard, occupying a large part of the land between Pleasantville and White Plains. I have heard it said that maundering old women find it depressing to ride the trains through Cemeteryland and try to concentrate on other things—such as the great literary works of Jacqueline Susann—while their train is in the Land of the Dead.

On the fringes of these cemeteries are the establishments of the tombstone people, who prefer to call themselves dealers in Monuments. One day when the New York train stopped at Kensico Cemetery Depot I took note of a monument-maker's workyard opposite my window. There were fragments of rare and excellent stone that had been hacked away in the fashioning of hundreds of gravestones. Right there I had my inspiration.

Up until the end of World War Two an outdoor "barbecue" was usually constructed by a mason, of flagstone perhaps, or whatever flattish stone might be available. Some people still prefer these masonry jobs over the portable types of charcoal broilers.

I planned a new one made of stone. I even drove down and got permission from the tombstone guys to gather fragments from their premises; I began picking up a few funereal shards each time I found myself driving in the vicinity of Cemeteryland. I accumulated a pile of the lovely sentimental rock and I sketched the form my barbecue would take. I knew I'd have a conversation piece potentially superior to the fireplaces of the Benninghoffs and Lowell Thomas.

There would be one important difference, however, over and above the fact that mine would be outdoors. I didn't plan on facing my guests, meat tongs in hand, pointing out each individual stone set into my structure and lecturing on its origin. I thanked Providence, in fact, that I didn't know a single thing about the parties buried beneath each of the tombstones from which my fragments came. I would never yammer about them and recite their obituaries. I couldn't do it if I wanted to. It would have been sufficient if I could just say in an offhand manner, "Oh, by the way, my fireplace here is built entirely out of chips and chunks hacked off of ten thousand tombstones." That'd start talk.

The project, alas, was never finished. It was never even started. The reason will appear later in this book.

TWELVE

I arrived at Alpine four days before The Confrontation and signed in at the Ponderosa Motor Hotel—a stopping place for tourists and a watering place for Alpine Society. X. Tolbert had begun the historic week with one of his better columns in which he argued that the airplane was invented in the town of Pittsburg, Texas, by a Texan—a Baptist preacher, no less—a full year before the Wright brothers flew at Kitty Hawk. This Texas inventor, the Reverend Burrell Cannon, said he found the formula for building an airplane in the Book of Ezekiel. I now realized that Tolbert was beyond the help of psychiatry and would probably soon be claiming that Wick Fowler originally stumbled upon cavier among the snub-nosed carp in Lake Austin near the State capital.

Subsequently X. Tolbert, having settled the origin of the airplane for all time to come,* published a boastful column saying that Texas has the second largest farkleberry tree in the world. He dug up an opinion out of a Dallas botanist named Dr. Cyrus Longworth Lundell who said, "I've never

---

* Later on I read in a Texas magazine that the world's first airplane was invented by Joseph Brodbeck, a Fredericksburg schoolteacher. This Brodbeck built his plane and flew it around the Hill country *thirty-eight* years before the Wright brothers got their craft off the ground at Kitty Hawk.

111

known any people who ate farkleberries." This man Tolbert belongs in the Big Time.

Preacher Cannon's Texas-bred airplane never left the ground but Tolbert said it could've. The Dallas hack should not be condemned for his columnar idiosyncrasies. Most Texans have the same twisted mentality when it comes to contemplating the glories of their State. As I write this solemn history, a Texan named Country Bill White has had himself buried alive in a grassy spot at the base of the screen of an Austin drive-in movie. Mr. White has had himself buried eight feet underground thirty times in his glowing career and he has contended that he is undisputed world's champion at this sort of frolic. He recently read in a London newspaper that an Irish bar-beast had gone underground in a coffin, seeking to shatter Country Bill's record. Country Bill promptly picked up his shovel and started digging. He issued a statement saying: "As soon as I heard this guy in London was a-gonna try to take the world's record away from me, I started making my arrangements. I had to keep that title not only for myself but for all of Texas. I love Texas." He is from Florida and in his spare time, when he is not busy loving Texas, he wrestles alligators.

Brewster County, wherein Alpine is the county seat, is the biggest of all the 254 counties in Texas. Its people, typically, enjoy telling you that the whole State of Connecticut would fit neatly within the boundaries of Brewster and some tack on the information that there would still be room for poor little Rhode Island. As everyone knows Rhode Island's greatest claim to distinction is that it is always being fitted inside other geographical areas; once the State had rough and ragged edges, but these have been worn down smooth from its being jigsawed into other places at home and abroad.

The people of Brewster County were agog over The Confrontation. The citizens of Alpine bowed to me on the street and addressed me as *El Exigente*—the discriminating one, the connoisseur, the sniffer of coffee beans. Newspapers throughout the State were, nonetheless, unleashing torrents of abuse against me, never letting up for a day. I retained my cool, a slightly derisive smile flickering on my lips.

There was mail awaiting me, and more coming in each day—letters from people supporting me in the forthcoming battle, and more letters from people calling me names, advising me to get lost.

There was a long telegram from Korczak Ziolkowski in Custer, South Dakota. This is the same Korczak Ziolkowski I mentioned a few pages back (could there be *another* Korczak Ziolkowski anywhere?). I first met Korczak during the same expedition on which I encountered the town of Alpine for the first time. He has been chopping and chiseling and bulldozing on that South Dakota mountain for nearly a quarter of a century. The image cut out of the mountain will be, if he ever gets it finished, 640 feet long and 563 feet high—a portrayal of Chief Crazy Horse astride a stallion, "riding the South Dakota skies like a gigantic specter of vengeance against injustices done his people," as Red Fenwick of Denver once phrased it.

Now Korczak had read of my single-handed war against the perfidious Texans and somehow, I guess, he got the idea that I am kin to the heroic Crazy Horse in character and personality. He wired good wishes and said that if I would batter Wick Fowler to the ground and win the contest, he would drop whatever he was doing and come to Texas and carve a likeness of me on the mountain of my choice.

I began shopping for a mountain at once. At first I decided that I would like to be on Paisano Mountain, between Alpine and Marfa—it stands beside U.S. 90 which is the main artery of travel westward toward California. I undertook a debate with myself whether I wanted to be full-face or in profile. Newspapermen from San Antonio and Austin and several other cities were already assembling in Alpine and some of them studied maps and booklets about the Big Bend country and offered suggestions. Hen Egg Mountain was mentioned, and Butcherknife Hill, and one correspondent simpered at me and suggested Capote Mountain. A man from Marathon got into the discussion and said there is a mountain down in Big Bend Park, a big one, known affectionately to menfolks in this area as Nellie's Tit. It is a perfectly rounded mountain, with the exact look of a woman's breast, and on the top, set precisely in the center, is a nipple. A most suitable mountain, said the Marathon man, for me to have my image carved upon. I said it would suit me, but that I could not permit the symmetry of the tit to be destroyed. Then Sam Wood of Austin came up with a photograph of Mule Ear Peaks, which he turned sideways and then pointed out that it looked like a profile of my head in a prostrate position—a position Mr. Wood said he had heard was not uncommon with me. He saw in the two Mule Ears my nose and my chin poked upward into the blue Texas sky. O, the hilarity of it! O, the jocosity! O, the rotten ways of newspaper drudges! I resolved to give this guy no scoops.

Also waiting for me in Alpine was a detailed account of a raging controversy that had broken out in Southern Illinois, the sward of my nativity. An old friend of mine, Charlie Feirich the Third, publisher of a newspaper in the Ohio River town of Metropolis, was engaged in a quarrel with a man named J. B. Humma. Their feud was a direct outgrowth of the dispute between Wick Fowler and myself.

Mr. Feirich writes a column in his own newspaper and he had produced an essay about the forthcoming doings at Terlingua. In his column he mentioned the fact that he was a chili-eater of some consequence, that he had but recently consumed three bowls of chili at a single sitting—chili he composed, incidentally, under my written direction.

This Mr. Humma challenged Mr. Feirich about the three

114

bowls and brought up the question of how much chili one bowl will hold, and then he multiplied that figure by three . . . being a brainy Illinois man. He said that Mr. Feirich had not done what he said he had done, and he described himself as a reader "who cannot be brainwashed by chili." Mr. Feirich, in a subsequent column, demonstrated his Methodist chagrin. He wrote:

Mr. Humma seems to be upset at my report that I ate three bowls of chili at one sitting. He goes on to indicate that a bowl must contain twelve ounces of liquid measure to qualify as a bowl and then insults me by declaring that I think of an egg cup as a bowl.

My chili bowl happens to be the same one I use for corn flakes. I had no thought of it meeting the Humma qualifications. I dug out a measuring cup which held eight ounces and discovered that my bowl holds more than the required Humma ounces. I didn't bother to check the ounces in an egg cup. . . . Mr. Humma's letter indicates that he does not believe I could eat three bowls of junket, and he's right. I have no recollection of ever eating junket in any quantity.

Humma claims that I am doing Illinois wrong and chili wrong by saying favorable things about Wick Fowler's famous 2-Alarm Chili. Humma has not tried 2-Alarm Chili and doesn't know what he is talking about. He reports that Taylor's Chili which is distributed from Carlinville, Illinois, is the best chili.

The Spin-off Chili War in Little Egypt went on from there, but it degenerated into a quarrel about the cubic capacity of bowls rather than the comparative goodness of various chilis, and I heard a report that Mr. Humma finally got so mad about Mr. Feirich's corn flakes bowl that he called Mr. Feirich out, and Mr. Feirich departed Metropolis in haste, having found assignments in Vacation Village, Florida, and later somewhere in distant Maine.

I wouldn't say that Charlie Feirich was supporting me with all the resources at his command, but from Las Vegas, Nevada, came word from an old friend, Sou Chan, offering moral support and actual physical help if I needed it. Mr. Chan is the dapper and delightful founder and present proprietor of the House of Chan restaurant just north of Times Square in Manhattan. Among all my acquaintances I believe Mr. Chan is the best talker as well as the best letter-writer. He is a Cantonese and came to the United States when he was eighteen and worked as a waiter in restaurants around Chicago and Milwaukee before traveling on to New York. He has become wealthy from his Manhattan restaurant and travels a great deal. He married a fine girl named Viola Eng and several years ago they sneaked away from their New York friends, disappearing without a word. A few weeks later they were back and Mr. Chan was ecstatic in describing a new and unknown place he had found. "They got," he told his pals, "a whole big thing over there cord Europe."

Chan's warm friends have included such notables as David Rockefeller, Rita Hayworth, Fred Allen, Freddie Woltman, and Lefty Gomez. Abe Savage once described Sou neatly, saying that "he approaches most of his problems with both the self-effacement of a gentle Chinese philosopher and the sharp gamin suspicion of a New York fight manager."

Chan's conversation occupies an entirely different plane than his English prose. He talks and writes at two levels, neither one resembling the other. There are delicate shadings in his talk. He managed to get me on the phone from Las Vegas where, he said, he was having much rucks. I have learned to understand his style of talk and knew that he was having much luck at the gaming tables. He was having so much rucks that he wouldn't be able to come to Terlingua and stand at my side while I cooked.

I have, in the past, jotted down facile phrases uttered by Chan. Once when he was trying to teach me some basic things about Chinese cooking, he grew irritated and said, "Oh, you dumb cruck!" Another time he was showing me through his Florida house. He flung open a door and said, "Nussing but utirrity room" and closed the door swiftly as if the utiritty room detracted somehow from the overall aesthetic attractiveness of his winter home. I once heard him tell a salesman, in his restaurant, to "Go fry a kite." I have heard him speak of "a terrible exprosion." He greets guests with, "Deerighted you could come." And he once snapped at his warm friend Freddie Woltman, "Quit foorin' aroun'!"

I had written Sou Chan in New York asking for any advice he might give me, for he is a culinary artist of great genius. I asked him if he had ever had any experience with chili, or with any kind of Mexican cookery; and I asked him how much time he had spent in Texas, and what his feelings were about the State.

Chan's mind sometimes wanders, and so does his English, when he sets himself at his typewriter to compose a letter. He sent me six pages of single-spaced, tightly written Chan prose and never once mentioned chili which, I was to learn later, he calls Mexico cherry, just as he is prone to cry out, "Ah-roe-ha!" when he goes to Hawaii. Here are some of the salient portions of his letter. Excuse me. *All* portions of all Chan letters are salient; it's simply that he writes at such length that I am unable to include it all.

You are so lucky on the trip Texas. All New Yorkers and those Westchester tycoons are freezing to dead this winter. I am sure you might have accidentally over heard in the radio since you don't read the most untrue newspaper anymore.

117

It sounds very exciting about your newly found ventures in cooking. I always like cooking my own food. not because I don't trust the other but I enjoy whatever the texture may be and even a poor flavor but my own which makes a great different in eating. I think all man should know how to cook but cook it with enthusiasm rather than open a freezer cabinet for a preprepared package.

Once I learned a recipe how to spoil a good Turkey, call "Mole De-Guajolote." I believed this recipe created long before the Texians learn to cook, but it has a certain amount of flavor of Texas method of cooking. but I will follow it up at the end of this letter. so some day you may like to try it when you have a Turkey that don't know what to do with. (He never did get back to that Turkey.)

Before you become a chef of any kind. I believe you should also know a bit about how to barbecue a whole pig, let say about 100 pounds enough feed a part of 100 people. I built a such an Oven. call Pig Oven. built it with red fire brick. 60 inches in diameter and five feet high. Inside the bottom of the Oven has a drip pan which occupied about 50 per cent of the space but the pan shaped like a half cocconut and a copper tube connected to the bottom of the pan so that the oil dripping would drop into the pan where the copper tube would carry the oil out of the oven wall and drop on a can outside of the oven. In feeding the heat into the oven, there is an opening on the side of the oven which extended about 20 inches where you can burn the wood or other fuel to heat the oven till 750 degree. or to make the wall of the oven inside so hot that you really don't need any more heat after you slip the pig into it.

As a toy I built one myself in the back yard of my house at Laurel Shore, Florida. The experience of that Barbecue party was an exciting one. If not bore you, you may be interest to read it as I try to describe as follow.

One day in late February last year. a good friend of ours David Dubinsky came and we went to give a party by having a dozen or two of our neighboring friends to join us. I thought of nothing better than to cook a whole pig for that.

So I went into a farm in near by make a deal with a farmer so that she willing to share one of her pig to me. It weights 85 pounds after dressed. Matter of fact, it is so heavy that have to have two farm hands lifted up and tied upon a tree before we able to cut open its stomach and clean thoroughly accordingly. It was a tough assignment because we had to cook the boiling water for the pig's hair on a huge wash tub put on a triangle cement block then feed the wood to make sure its skin like a baby's fanny. We brought the pig home and applied the preprepared candiment on the inside of the pig and let it marinate for six hours or longer. while marinating the pig with the seasoning goodies. two hour prior to the pig getting into the oven, start the fire and keep feeding it until the flame are highest heat the fuel can be produced. of course, must let the lid of the oven open a little so that the air able to circulate to let the heat go around inside the oven heat all around the walls of the bricks. then slip the pig into. Have an irion bar resting across the top of the oven and hang the pig onto the bar then cover the lid and let it hang there for about one hour. while doing that must let the bottom of the fire feeding hole open a little so that the air can circulate to let the heat go up. Then pull the pig out after an hour. Use an ice pick, with one fist holding the ice pick but only let the sharp point out from the hand about an inch then keep plucking to the pig's skin with the sharp point of the ice pick till all the skin are evenly plucking the holes onto about every 2 inches in distance. the other words, drill a hole onto the pig's skin on every 2 inch space. the purpose of this is to let the pig fat out when the heat heats to the skin after apply a several coats of honey and salt and water mixed. the other words again, before pull the pig out from the oven, you should prepare a big bucket of one pound honey, half pound salt and one gallion boiling water, mixed it well then used chees cloth dip into mixture and apply on the skin of pig after punch the holes on the skin. this would let the mixture get into the skin when the pig return into the oven. the heat heats the skin, then the oil start to come out from those hole and drop onto the dripping pan and out to

119

the can outside of the oven. while you doing that. perhaps needs to give more heat because the oven getting cold while in motion from all the above process which often let more heat escape from the oven. therefore, it is good to start more fire while the pig inside. but make sure the flame not hitting the skin because there is enough space in the bottom of the oven to let the heat arise. all you need is to start the fire on the edge of the fire feeding tube which I meantion 20 inches from the wall of the oven where the opening is at. Perhaps my upsidown English is confucis you. but with your intelligent, I am sure you can make it out what I mean. . . .

It goes on from there for three more single-spaced pages and I would include the entire recipe except that I haven't been able to adapt it to the cooking of a pot of chili. I puzzled over it, but I can't see the need of that big structure with the fire feeding hole and letting the sharp point of the ice pick out from the hand to keep plucking until all the skin are evenly plucking the holes into every 2 inches in distance. Moreover, I got no copper tube for dripping of oil. One significant fact I found in the Chan prescription, however, is that indubitably, Wick Fowler's chili is preprepared.

I cannot leave Sou Chan without giving you his advice to young women who might be searching for "the ideal man." Years ago Chan toyed with the idea of founding "a specialized go-betwin service" which would furnish lovely girl friends for men. Chan drew up a list of rules and procedures which he felt young lady clients should follow if they wanted him to find a good man for them. I think the procedures apply just as well today and I offer them to any female customers I may have:

"short-cut to marry" as follow . . .
1. have a freshly haircut.
2. done the hair so not like a jidgiburg stage girl (home girl manner better)

120

3. white blouse but not a heavy print.
4. conservative black suit.
5. no hat preferable.
6. no perfume positively.
7. don't paint your finger nail if you haven't.
8. don't overdone your face with powder.
9. never order more than three drinks at first time out.
10. put your enthusiasm when baby subject brought up. The other word, you must love kids.
11. try not to order the most expensive item on menu.
12. don't over fed yourself as all man like delicate stomach girl.
13. try not to look at HIM when you talk but must show your *sweetness* and *charming* eye.
14. don't take the floor all yourself, encourage HIM talk more. only way to find out things.
15. most likely HE will touch you, but let him. only for 2 seconds. repules him gently and looking at his face with smile at the same time.
16. don't agree all what he said even you do, to demand respect.
17. eat slowly, and don't be a dishwasher because no man like see HER as a hog.
18. talk slowly, give a timely smile, don't show your anziety, terpermental is out.
19. don't talk what fashion you like, talk something he like once a while.
20. admire HIS appearance when chance arrived but only on clothing and ties not his face or feature because no man like to tell him is handsome direct by his girl.

The other word, you must be tactfull all time. good luck to you there is all yours.

Truly yours,
Per SOU CHAN
Match Consultant.

Nothing in there about chili, nothing about Texas, but I told you in the beginning that I planned to follow the

121

Durant method of writing history; the exploits of Sou Chan fit into that pattern and, in fact, would fit into any pattern. Because of him I never intend to order more than three drinks at first time out, even if I'm consorting with a jidgiburg stage girl.

THIRTEEN

On the morning of 19th October a fresh bulletin was spewn forth from the headquarters of the Dallas camarilla. Someone called The Committee had issued a ruling that everyone attending the Terlingua tournament should wear khakis and hunting jackets. Committees do not advise me how to dress, no more than how and where I should sleep. I had already chosen my cooking costume—a wine red basketweave sports jacket from Tripler on Madison Avenue, expensive as hell; light blue sports shirt and powder blue slacks run up by Forchheimer's of Alpine, and a sweat shirt designating me as a high school halfback.

The Chili Appreciation Society had already sent me a thing described as a "chili bib" with the customary inane lettering on it. I rejected it instantly, advising the high command of the CASI that "in my set we do not slobber and drool our chili."

The ukase from Dallas also indicated that no matter how big the crowd at Terlingua, Wick Fowler and I would prepare enough chili to feed everyone. I dashed off a telegram to the Society, threatening to pick up my tools and depart. I told them: "I have no intention of engaging in a wholesale slopping of Texas hawgs."

This message had no more than left my hand when my

attention was called to a muddy automobile pulling in at the Ponderosa. It stopped, and separated into two parts, indistinguishable one from the other, and one half of it moved, and entered Room 24.

About an hour later I descried a large man standing near the swimming pool strumming his lips in a lighthearted manner. I watched him, fascinated, and thought that at any moment he might take a dead mouse out of his pocket and begin fondling it and talking to it. I approached him and introduced myself to him—he was the part of the muddy automobile that had moved. He made some Austin-type noises, consisting of vague statements about politics, sternwheelers, and cookery. This was my first meeting with Wickford P. Fowler. Newspaper people, swiftly recognizing the epic quality of the encounter, began flocking from all quarters and Mr. Fowler spoke.

"My chili," he said, "has been known to open up eighteen sinus cavities unknown to modern medicine."

I kept matters on a genteel plane and said, simply and modestly, "I'll cook you blue in the face, you big ox."

The newspaper people felt that this first meeting of the contestants called for a fiesta, a midday banquet, and so all of us retired to "The Club"—an institution connected with the motel where the gentlemen of the press had been keeping the cocktail waitresses on the hop. "The Club" is one of those peculiar institutions which reflect the wisdom and hideous hypocrisy of the Texas liquor laws. I walked beside Mr. Fowler and there was hostility in the air, for he said to me, "I'm thinking about cooking against you with one hand tied behind my back." I responded, "If Nature had furnished you with four arms, sir, you still would not be able to churn butter." We all filed in and took places at a long table and had a fine feast. Of whisky.

I tried to ascertain what The Committee had in mind

when it prescribed the method by which the judges were to be selected. Mr. Fowler was to pick *his* judge, I was to choose one for myself, and there would be a "neutral" judge—Maury Maverick, Jr. Neutral! Bull droppings! A turncoat, a renegade, a lifelong citizen of San Antonio in the State of Texas, the man who attacked me very near as bitterly as Ole X. Tolbert. I couldn't understand how two contestants in a cooking duel could each pick a judge and Mr. Fowler assured me he couldn't understand it either, but he added that he was "going to the bridge" with his two hundred and nine backers.

He said he had brought me some special chili-cooking equipment in case I needed it, and we retired to his quarters. He brought out of his room a brand new iron pot which he said was the same size as his own aluminum pot, plus a wooden stirring paddle a yard long. Then he handed me a package of Wick Fowler's 2-Alarm Chili mix, and smirked egregiously, quite a feat in itself. I noted a group of press photographers in a huddle nearby and so I flang the pre-prepared chili to the gravel. The photographers rushed up and had me fling it to the gravel three more times. They said it was a picture that would make Page One.

Mr. Fowler told me that the present head of the Chili Appreciation Society would not be able to attend at Ter-lingua, on account of some business deal he had going in the East. I was sorry about this because I wanted to meet Mr. George Haddaway, the Chief Chili-Head of Dallas. I wanted to meet the man who is so dedicated to Texas-style chili that one day in 1936 he committed a physical assault upon the chef of a restaurant in Houston's International Airport—the man had put Boston baked beans in Mr. Haddaway's order of chili. Mr. Haddaway was so incensed that he attacked the chef, kneeing him in the groin, and police came on the run. Mr. Haddaway explained about the Boston baked beans in his chili, and the cops began glaring at the villainous chef, and fingering their nightsticks. Mr. Haddaway was not prosecuted for the crotch assault; it was said at the time that even if they had changed the venue to the far borders of Texas, still no jury would have convicted him. The second reason I wanted to meet Mr. Haddaway was that someone told me he was sore because nobody had sent him a free copy of *Holiday*.

I decided to be straightforward with Mr. Fowler in the promotional aspects of the contest. A man named Calvin Clyde, Jr., wrote in his newspaper, the Tyler *Courier-Times*, that "The 'feud' between Fowler and Smith is a phony. It is mostly a publicity thing, to keep Smith's name known to the postmen who have to track him down in delivering his pension check, and to help Fowler sell boats. Actually, Smith knows nothing about chili and while Fowler cooks it well enough to dull off the appetites of free loaders of the Greater Dallas variety, he never eats his own cooking. To tell the truth, Fowler prefers the chili I make, usually from deer meat, or that turned out by his brother Ike."

Much of the publicity stuff had been coming from the offices of a big public relations outfit in "Greater" Dallas, a firm headed by a man named Tom Tierney. What were they publicizing? Mr. Fowler said he didn't think they were trying to promote anything—that they were doing it all for fun. I said horse doodles. There was a honkey in the woodpile somewhere.

My opponent and I mixed around together the rest of the day and unaccountably began to enjoy one another's company. The newspaper guys were being convivial. There were new arrivals with each passing hour, and I can remember, among others, Garth Jones of the AP, Kyle Thompson of the UPI (both being head men for their wire services in Texas), Sam Wood of the *Austin American-Statesman*, Art Leibson

126

of the El Paso *Times,* Jim Curran of the Houston *Chronicle,* Harley Pershing of the Fort Worth *Star-Telegram,* and nobody from the Houston *Post.* When I met Jim Curran and George Honeycutt from the Houston *Chronicle* Wick Fowler remarked that the *Chronicle* plant is on Travis Street, named for Gregory L. Travis, inventor of the suspender button. The Austin *American-Statesman* had more than Sam Wood on the scene. I also met, from that paper, Bill Woods, the city editor, founder of the Midland Yacht Club up in the greasy prairie country of West Texas, and Nat Henderson, who has been mentioned before. Mr. Henderson is Prince Seal of the Royal Seals of the Melanesian Archipelago, an organization founded in 1944 at the site of the Mission Nuestra Senora Del Espiritu Santo de Zuniga in Goliad, Texas. The mission was founded to convert the Karankawa Indians, who were ferocious cannibals. Texas newspapermen are fraught with interest. I must not forego mentioning the presence, also, of Ormly Gumfudgin of the *Wretched Mess News,* West Yellowstone, Montana. That's the way Ormly Gumfudgin identified himself, and he looked it.

It was one of the Austin boys who informed me that the Chili Appreciation Society was sending one of its members, a Dallas rabbi, to Terlingua. He was coming with his skinning knife and some photographs of me (head photos) and with instructions about what to do. "If he approaches me," I said, "I will scuffle with him."

That day's mail brought stacks of stuff. Included was a handsome calling card with the name of Lyndon B. Johnson on it, the engraved lettering and seal sticking up like crossbar piecrust, and on the back, written in ink: "Dear H. Allen: This is to certify that you know more about chili than I do. Lyndon." The postmark was Pleasantville, N.Y. And someone sent a column by Matt Weinstock of the Los Angeles *Times.* Mr. Weinstock reported that a young woman

127

walked into a Montebello market and asked where she could find the corn pads. She was directed to the drug department. A minute later she was back. "Not that ky-yund," she said in a rich Texas accent. "Ah mean th' ky-yund uh cawn pads y'all put ground meat on um and eat um." Tortillas.

A debonair citizen of Alpine, Attorney John E. Allen, called on me and presented me with a chili recipe printed on a card. I assumed that Mr. Allen passes out these cards as a means of engendering good will. His recipe originated in the Dallas County prison system. Much has been said and much written about Texas jail chili. Some Texans consider it to be the greatest of all chilis. In case you are interested in felon food, here it is:

½ pound or 2 cups ground beef suet.
2 pounds ground beef.
3 buds garlic.
1½ tbsps. paprika.
3 tbsps. chili powder.
1 tbsp. comino seed.
1 tbsp. salt.
1 tsp. white pepper.
1½ finely diced dried sweet chile pods.
3 cups water.

Fry out suet in heavy kettle. Add meat, finely diced garlic, and seasonings; cover. Cook slowly 4 hours, stirring occasionally. Add water; continue cooking about 1 hour until slightly thickened. Serve plain or mixed with equal portions of cooked dried pink or red beans. Serves 6. (Dried chile pods may be omitted.)

I overdid in thanking Mr. Allen, because later on he presented me with his recipe for making Texas sourdough, a long and involved and intricate procedure that makes Sou Chan's recipe for stuck pig sound like frying an egg.

It was Nat Henderson who furnished me with details of the new uprising in San Antonio. The Chamber of Commerce in that city had suddenly come to life, greatly alarmed over the fact that Terlingua was being widely described as the Chili Capital of the World. An emergency decree was hustled together and David Straus, president of the Chamber, mobilized the T. E. F. (Terlingua Expeditionary Force) for the invasion of the ghost town. Straus ordered the T. E. F. to "move on Terlingua with all possible speed and take whatever measures are necessary to protect San Antonio's reputation as the Chili Capital of the World."

Floyd O. Schneider, an executive of the Lone Star Brewing Company, who was planning to fly a planeload of his beer to Terlingua anyway, was made Commander in Chief of the T. E. F. According to Nat Henderson, there seemed to be no hope of mediation of the deteriorating relations between Terlingua and San Antonio, and Commander in Chief Schneider was faced with a precarious logistical situation—the Budweiser people were offering assistance to Terlingua with a liberal giveaway aid program.

Wick Fowler got busy on the phone in an effort to save the situation. He leaked news to the San Antonio papers that the City Council of Terlingua was willing to make certain concessions to maintain peace. He suggested that the two parties to the dispute meet somewhere and try to decide on a place to meet. "Terlingua," he said, "is willing to let San Antonio have the HemisFair if it will relinquish all claims to being Chili Capital of the World."

This was all most edifying to me; the Little Entente members were quarreling bitterly among themselves. Commander in Chief Schneider lost his head completely and announced that when the T. E. F. marched into Terlingua, gonfalons flying, by god they would *seize* something. When asked to particularize on what they would seize, he stammered a bit, then said, "We'll seize whatever is there." Someone told him, "But there ain't anything there." Whereupon this pipsqueak caudillo said, "Then by god we'll *take* something there!"

All of this hullabaloo convinced me that the total collapse of American civilization was imminent. I remembered reading, a few days earlier, in a Texas magazine, a letter from a subscriber which seemed to be typical of almost all letters-to-the-editor. A citizen of Nacogdoches was sored up about the universal dishonesty of television repairmen, and wrote: "What kind of rot has set into this country? How long will it be before we sink quietly into the sea?" My sentiments, exactly. I spoke my feelings to Harley Pershing. "You people," I said, "are out of the mainstream. You are not even in the crick. With a paddle." His response was abrupt: "I pay no nevermind to Yankee talk. Ever."

I went to my room with the intention of taking a nap but I got to looking at the iron pot Wick Fowler had brought me. I remembered that an iron pot has to be seasoned before it is used the first time. If I hauled that pot down to Terlingua and cooked in it, my chili would come out as black as two yards down a bull's throat and tasting like the Mesabi Range in Minnesota. Then there was the odor, a faint aroma that wasn't new iron. I now recalled that I had given my formula for sassatate to certain individuals in East Texas at the time I discovered, or invented sassatate, last year. I sniffed the pot. Rubbed my fingers around in it. I felt certain that someone had impregnated this pot with essence of sassatate, but it was not *good* sassatate. It was unsaturated pollywise. I must explain that the principal use of sassatate, in its pure form, is to sore up the feet of kitchen cockroaches and impel them to head for the tules. It is not good in chili.

130

I took the pot downtown and conferred with Mrs. Paul Forchheimer, one of the town's better cooks. She told me that she had an iron pot at home the same size as the booby-trapped Fowler pot, and that I could foil him and his dastardly scheme by using the Forchheimer utensil. He'd never know the difference. As it turned out, he never did.

Mr. Fowler told me he had heard that I had some secret ingredient I planned to use at Terlingua. I assured him this was true and let him have a glimpse of it. Before I left New York a letter had come from Richard Bradford, who lives in Santa Fe, New Mexico. I have known Dick since he was a boy in New Orleans, the son of Roark and Mary Rose Bradford. He had written me:

I enjoyed your piece on chili in *Holiday* although your inclusion of tomatoes in the recipe is open to question. Julie's recipe is very similar to yours. She generally uses both ground beef and cubed lean pork.

If you want to use already powdered chile, and not go through the business of making your own pulp from the pepper (which is a pain in the ass but authentic), you must use only the finest, purest powdered chile. Depending on the variety, it may be mild, hot, very hot, or exquisitely painful, but it must be of a high quality. . . . That dark red goop that the spice makers call "chili powder" is pretty nasty. For one thing, it is adulterated with other stuff, including stale herbs and spices and probably shredded paper.

In the Rio Grande Valley of northern New Mexico we grow what are, in my opinion, the finest and most flavorful chiles in the world. I am sending you a small package of finely ground Chimayo red chile, of a medium hotness. Please understand, I'm not suggesting you change your favorite recipe in any way. *Chacun a son chili,* as Cardinal Richelieu used to say. I'm just offering you a few hundred grains of earthly paradise. Use it as you do your present brand of chili powder, and them rich neighbors of yours will be sitting on your doorstep whimpering for admittance.

New Mexico is still, I maintain, the best source of ground or powdered chile, which grows handsomely in the Española, Pojoaque, Nambé, and lower Rio Grande valleys. There are forty-eleven varieties, and a dedicated *cocinero de chiles* like yourself may blend them to your fancy in the privacy of your kitchen. Anyone like Mr. Wick (is that his name?) who would use a prepackaged mix is obviously approaching the problem with a trivial attitude, and can do nothing but debase the art. I can tell from his picture that he's neither ascetic nor dedicated, both necessary qualities. In that rowdy group, only your face had the proper expression of restraint and saintly suffering, something like Simon Stylites with a buzz on.

The Chimayo stuff arrived. I took two plastic vials, of the kind that pills come in nowadays, washed them out, and funneled in *two* secret ingredients. One vial contained a special brand of powdered cumin that I had been using lately. I took my labeling machine and labeled it, "Powdered Rattlesnake Urine," just to confuse secret agents from the other side. I then filled another vial with Dick Bradford's Chimayo chile powder, which I labeled "Shredded Coyote Whammadoodle—Red Part." These two vials fitted neatly into a glass jar I had, which I labeled "OYAMIHC." When people asked, I would say it was a Comanche Indian word. Actually it was "Chimayo" spelled backward.

After dinner the proprietor of an Alpine restaurant approached me and told me that "you and this Fowler bird can holler all you wanta, but they got the wrong cooks cookin' at Terlingua Sattaday." He assured me that he, personally, creates the best chili in all Christendom. One of his secrets, he said, is to use plenty of grease. "Never skin the grease offen chili," he added. He favors plenty of garlic—two or three times as much garlic as most ree-seets call for. I told him that I had not seen chili mentioned on his bill of fare and he admitted he never serves it in his place. "Too greazy," he said. "Gets the pans all greazy, gets the cook greazy, gets the waitresses greazy, and sometimes it gets the customers greazy. Not worth the trouble."

This man, I decided, was not a true aficionado.

I bade Wick Fowler good night without insulting him. I simply said, "*Hasta mañana,* gristle-eater." He showed me a telegram from Washington, signed by correspondents assigned to the White House. They said they stood "four square and four alarm behind you in this cook-off with that confused Yankee upstart who calls his tomato soup chili." I spread their insolent names on the record: Jack Sutherland, Jack Horner, Duff Thomas, Merriman Smith, Bob Young, Stan Carter, Oscar Griffin, Muriel Dobbins, Jessie Stern, Frank Cormier, and Bob Pierpont. The motive of their telegram was obvious to me the moment I saw it. They spend all of their spare time licking the President's posterior.

Our chili tournament now has *everything* going for it. It is whole and complete. A racist angle has been injected into the picture. A gentleman named Jose L. Ortiz, Jr., has written to the papers complaining that no Mexican-American has been named to the panel of judges or to anything else in the Terlingua contest. Senor Ortiz forgot one important question. What would a Mexican-American know about chili?

FOURTEEN

On the day prior to The Confrontation there was excitement in the crisp Alpine air. When I opened the door of my room at the Ponderosa there was a package on the stoop, and a note. The note said: "Senor Smeeth I geeve you geeft for to beat them puerco cochino puto sawn a beech from Dallas." My training as a linguist and as a student of dialects led me to suspect the authenticity of the message.

The package was a plastic baggie containing about a pound of dry beans. There was something about them that looked dangerous. I took them down the road a half mile to Sul Ross College where agriculture is a large subject and the professors identified them for me. They were *fava* beans from the Mediterranean. Eating one *fava* bean, or merely inhaling its aroma or pollen, is likely to bring on vertigo, nausea, polevault vomiting (performed in a parabola), and sometimes utter collapse. There is at the same time a massive destruction of the red blood cells. The professors of bean farming told me that if the Chili Appreciation Society was responsible for leaving the *favas* at my doorstep, I could have the entire membership imprisoned if not electrocuted. I chose the way of patience. I bode my time.

Upon returning to the motel I found that the villainous X. Tolbert had arrived late the night before from Dallas. I had no way of knowing if he . . . I could not make an accusation re beans. Wick Fowler, who was preparing to shove off for Terlingua, introduced me to Tolbert who was costumed as if he were about to undertake a supporting role in the filming of "Nanook of the North." He seemed surly, sinister, and mentally disturbed. I, on the other hand, was almost courtly in my show of manners in the presence of this man. He and Fowler wanted to know if I needed a sleeping bag or bedroll—they had come with extras. I said I was going to spend the coming night in a comfortable bed right where I was.

"You don't seem to be showing the proper spirit," said X. "The rest of us are going to rough it down at the ranch." I responded that I have no taste for such foolishness, that I got that sort of thing out of my system real fast when I was a Boy Scout, that I had no intention of sleeping in some primeval slum. I led Tolbert over to Wick Fowler's car and pointed to its contents. In addition to all his pots and pans there were two single mattresses, a Harvard bedframe (reinforced), a set of box springs, three pillows, a battery-powered bedlamp, and, get this, a chemical commode.

"All he needs," I told Tolbert, "is an electric back scratcher and a place to plug it in."

"Our man," said Tolbert, "has to keep in good condition."

"He should have started way earlier," I said, and added, "forty years earlier."

Fowler took off southward, toward the high mountains and the Rio Grande, accompanied by Kyle Thompson of United Press International. Tolbert disappeared in the direction of Marfa, probably looking for records to show that the cotton gin was invented at Presidio. Also the sewing machine.

I went to the courthouse in Alpine to call on the Justice of the Peace, Mrs. Hallie Stillwell. Mrs. Stillwell is one of the great characters of Brewster County and West Texas. She came to Alpine early in the century in a covered wagon. She is a historian of the Big Bend country and has worked in collaboration with Virginia Madison, who is one of the leading writers with a strong interest in the region. I wanted to ask Mrs. Stillwell for some information about Terlingua. She proved to be a charming and intelligent woman.

"Since you are staying out at the Ponderosa," she said, "perhaps you can answer a question for me. All of a sudden Alpine is being overrun by a lot of men who have a sort of criminal look about them. I noticed some of them slinking and skulking around the Ponderosa when I was out there yesterday, and now they are beginning to appear on the downtown streets. Do you know who they are?"

"They are people from Dallas and Austin and San Antonio, mostly Dallas," I said. "I don't think they are outright criminals, though I don't trust any of them."

"A strange thing," said Mrs. Stillwell. "Since I've noticed them around town, for the first time in forty-five years I've started locking my car whenever I leave it anywhere."

There was something about this woman that I liked. A person of judgment and perception. Impulsively I asked her if she would serve as my judge in the chili contest. She said it didn't sound right, that someone should serve as *my* judge. I said, "Those dirty criminals from Dallas have appointed *their* judge." Mrs. Stillwell then wanted to know what the assignment would entail and I said I didn't know, but there wouldn't be any physical labor connected with it. She accepted the appointment and I said she could ride to Terlingua with me the next morning.

I then said: "These roughnecks we were discussing are the people who are against me. Some of them are newspapermen, but their monopolistic bosses have instructed them to bear down on me. The Chili Appreciation Society is bitter toward me because I have had the temerity to challenge their superiority, and because I am from New York, and I think they might resort to violence. They are desperate and crummy men. There are two hundred and nine of the sons of . . . of them. I think I ought to wear a gun. Would it be legal, and do you know where I can get a real hawg-leg with gunbelt and holster?"

"I think I know the exact place to get you a good six-gun," she said. "One with an honorable history. I'll get busy on it at once."

Hallie Stillwell, in addition to being a public official and a writer, still operates a cattle ranch a far shot south of Marathon, is Alpine correspondent for a couple of city newspapers, writes a column on ranching for the Alpine *Avalanche,* and serves as mother superior to a whole horde of people in Alpine who have foggy noodles and need some-one to lead them in out of the rain. She told me a lot about Terlingua . . . please keep in mind, I still had not seen the town.

I returned to the Ponderosa and began sorting out my notes concerning Wick Fowler. Know your opponent. Seek out his weaknesses. Analyze his chili.

Fowler attained his greatest notoriety as a war correspon-dent for Texas papers, though he had been a city detective in Austin and a Texas highway patrolman in his earlier years. In World War II he covered campaigns in Italy, France, and Germany, then in the South Pacific. He was aboard the U.S.S. *Missouri* when the Japs surrendered, and he was one of the first three newspapermen to enter Hiro-shima after the atomic bomb attack on that city. He has worked for newspapers in Austin, Dallas, Midland, and Denton.

Somewhere back yonder I mentioned X. Tolbert's column about the invention of the airplane by a Baptist preacher in Texas. I'm sure Wick Fowler believes that to be true. He is a Texan and Texans believe. Texans believe anything and everything. Revealed religion is not enough for them—they wear *it* to sickly shreds in their devotion to it and then they go looking for additional things to believe in. I remember a Chicago newspaperman describing for me his wife's incessant involvement with religion. "She believes things," he said, "that a mud turtle would blush to believe." An apt description of the frightened condition of the average Texan. He goes whole hog for the astrology crap, table levitation, the Bishop Pike-style hallucinations in which dear ones speak from The Beyant, reincarnation in which people die and come back to earth as goats and United States senators and crawdads and folk singers. Newspapermen in Texas believe in the power of prayer, and professors go to church and sing hymns. The first time I ever heard of a flying saucer was during a tour of Texas nearly a quarter of a century ago; the thing had been sighted over Del Rio by a half-witted grease monkey, and every man, woman, and child in Del Rio believed. It is my impression that if you turned up anywhere in West Texas and challenged water-witching, you would be knocked down in the street.*

Wick Fowler believes in the power of prayer but he is also a scientist and a social philosopher. For several years he has been pestering the City Council of Austin asking that a law be passed making it a crime for a criminal to leave the scene of a crime.

He told me that one of the chief troubles in the world today is the "inability gap" in chili-making. I suspect, however, that Mr. Fowler suffers under an inability gap of his own when it comes to other kinds of cooking. The only recipe I've ever heard him mention, other than his chili, is

---

* Another folk belief that is pervasive is this: nobody ever dies; there is no death. Everybody *passes away*. Says the Texas widow: "It's ben four year since he passed away." Sometimes they don't pass away, they pass on. In Texas when they talk about how Jesse James was brought down by Bob Ford, they say that Jesse passed on. Hitler passed away in that Chancellery bunker in 1945. King Kong, machine-gunned on the Empire State building, passed away.

the formula for boiling water, set forth earlier in this book. He has a brother, Ike Fowler, who is more to my liking as a cook. Ike Fowler is no one-dish man. He has won high honors in the Pillsbury Bake-Off, competing against female women, and he is celebrated around Austin for such things as his hot potato salad and something called "Papa's Golden Smash Brown Potato Hills." I'd rather cook against Ike Fowler than against Wick; after all, I can do other things than cook chili. I'd like for Wick to taste my orange-glazed duck, or hear me play the electrified organ, or taste the zucchini I grow.

There are areas, however, in which an observer might detect a kinship between Wick and me. He is an inventor. He is working on a square fishing reel which gives the line a little jerk as it turns the corners; it is for bass fisherman who feel they have to give their line little jerks to attract the fish. Another Fowler invention is the bifocal scope for the guns of bear hunters. Wick points out that a bear hunter usually shoots his grizzly at a distance of a hundred yards or more; invariably the bear picks himself up, takes offense, and goes for the hunter. When he gets within ten feet of his man, he can be clearly positioned in the lower part of the bifocal scope and brought down.

I was delighted to discover that Mr. Fowler has had thoughts about that butter bean in the Alamo. Some years ago I was in the San Antonio shrine and saw the white butter bean in a gold-framed case, lying on a bed of cotton, somewhat withered in appearance. I learned that this was the sole surviving butter bean from an almost forgotten episode in the glorious history of Texas. It was one of the Perote butter beans. Way back yonder 173 Texans who had been imprisoned by Santa Anna in Perote Prison escaped. They were recaptured and Santa Anna ordered that every tenth one be shot. One hundred and seventy-three beans were put into a pot; seventeen of them were black, the rest were white. The prisoners were blindfolded and compelled to draw beans. Those who drew the black ones were marched right out into the yard and shot.

Now, the Alamo is administered by the Daughters of the Republic of Texas, an organization of women similar to the Daughters of the American Revolution, though somewhat more patriotic. There is a big desk near the main entrance to the Alamo and usually several of these Daughters may be found there; they are, for the most part, rather grim and forbidding looking, but this is understandable when we take into consideration the fact that the weight of history, Texas history, presses down upon them like an incubus and they don't drink.

I approached a couple of these Daughters that day and putting on my most studious air, identified myself as a leading chili cook of New York. I said I was thinking about moving to Texas, but I hadn't as yet been able to make the final decision. I asked them if they would allow me to open that case in the other room and take out that white bean and take it home with me and cook it in a bowl of chili and then eat the chili. I said that such a procedure, I was sure, would put the true feel of Texas into my bloodstream and I would have no difficulty in deciding about moving to Texas.

Those ladies were horrified, and their eyes bugged out, and I could tell they believed they had a Yankee madman on their hands. I didn't give them a chance to pull themselves together, or to call for the Texas Rangers. I simply faded quickly into the crowd and left them with a new historical episode to narrate at the next meeting of the Daughters.

Now Wick Fowler told me that he knew about that butter bean, and that he had long entertained the notion of getting a group of night-riding members of the Chili Appreciation Society together for a raid on the Alamo, the sole purpose of which would be to shatter the glass of the gold-framed case, take out the white butter bean, and place in its stead a hand-

140

some Texas pinto bean. "I always felt," said Mr. Fowler, "that it was one hell of a note—if somebody's got to kill a Texan they ought to let him draw something better than a butter bean."

As a final tribute to Mr. Fowler, I would like to call attention to an honor that had recently come to him. He showed me a letter he had received from Dayton, Ohio, on the engraved stationery of the Chickenshit Athletic Club. The letter was inspired by the wide publicity accorded The Great Confrontation at Terlingua, but the crummy bastards in Dayton didn't nominate *me* to membership. The letter said in its printable part:

"Our membership in the Chickenshit Athletic Club consists of some twenty-odd broken-down athletic buffs who meet each Sunday during the fall months for a sociable brew and stew as we coach and referee the Cleveland Browns games. Our spring activities consist of an annual trek to the Bourbon Open, in Bardstown, Kentucky, where the amber fluid flows from the middle faucet, and the golf is merely an adjunct to the occasion. We also sponsor an annual Chickenshit Golf Tournament at a Dayton club."

As I say, I didn't get invited in. Oh well, you can't garner all the world's honors. I was happily able to inform Mr. Fowler that I was once a member of the Son-of-a-Bitch Club in San Bernardino, California, and while I was away in the South Pacific, unable to defend myself, a meeting was held at which I was voted unworthy. I was expelled.

FIFTEEN

Texas is where they play big league baseball in the house, a commonwealth whose citizens have answers to all questions, and alibis for every seeming fault. A gentleman named Jack Hodgens, out of Odessa, called on me at the motel to discuss a business matter and since my whole adult life has been one of snooping and prying in the interest of great literature, I began asking him questions. Mr. Hodgens is from Oklahoma and there has always been hearty animosity and belligerence between Oklahoma and Texas, yet he has managed to adapt and, in a way, has become sufficiently fond of Texas to root insanely for the Dallas Cowboys football team.

I told Mr. Hodgens that I might win out over Wick Fowler on the strength of meat alone. In a gentle and cautious manner I spoke to Mr. Hodgens of the consistent wiriness of Texas beef. I declared that several times I have tried a serving of the widely popular horror, the chicken-fried steak. It is strictly for half-soling shoes.

I asked the man from Odessa to explain, in simple terms, why it is that Texans are unable to lay their hands on good meat—Texas, the Meat State.

"I suppose," Mr. Hodgens said, "that it's because Texans

like tough meat. I believe they *like* to have a certain amount of sinewy gristle because it makes them feel manly. I wouldn't be surprised to see a Texan send a steak back to the kitchen with the complaint that it ain't *leathery* enough. Now," Mr. Hodgens went on, "I can tell you something more. I have got into the habit of enjoying tough meat since I moved to Texas. I like all my food to have some body to it; I like it to fight back. *I happen to like tough waffles.*"

I regarded him with incredulity. Tough waffles. Maybe the church people are right and the Day of Perdition is close at hand.

"I was in Miami Beach not long ago," said Mr. Hodgens, "and I went in a diner to get some waffles. I didn't want any of these damn feeble waffles that they say melt in your mouth, no more than I'd want a steak that melts in your mouth. The short order cook was a rough-looking customer with a bent ear, and I said to him, 'You know how to make tough waffles?' He just nodded. Didn't grin. Didn't see anything unusual in the question. And he made 'em. Tough. Tough as hell. He knew. So after I had the first bite and got it ground down, I said to him, 'You happen to be from Texas?' He nodded again. It figured."

At the Ponderosa someone handed me several sheets of verse composed by Eck Bludsoe, described as the Poet Laureate of the Chili Appreciation Society. Poet Bludsoe writes his stuff to the rhythm of other poets. Here is one he composed in the manner of Joyce Kilmer:

> *No person shall I ever see*
> *Who is addicted as is me;*
> *Addicted to the Fowler Chili,*
> *I eat it daring, willy-nilly,*
> *Then steel myself for what must come,*
> *That fiery exit through my bum.*

Scans. Lyrical in a way. I read the rest of Mr. Bludsoe's poems which were composed in honor of the Terlingua Confrontation. They were, in the main, directed against me when they were not celebrating "fruity farts" and other types of flatus. I thought this wind-breaking aspect of the Bludsoe verse quite surprising. I have been under the impression that Texas men, though their backside trumpetings be audible from Dallas to El Paso, would never admit to having any digestive disorder as a consequence of eating fiery chili. Especially any gaseous disorder. I mean, of course, any gaseous disorder in the region of the bum. Elsewhere doesn't count.

Eck Bludsoe, in his lyrics, doesn't give sex much of a play though he has produced a saucy poem done in the manner of Poe's *The Raven*. This tender ballad tells of a gentleman arriving home to find . . .

> *There they lay, totally nude,*
> *With the sweet happy smile of the totally screwed.*
> *The two of them lay there, without any shame,*
> *The man couldn't even tell me his name.*
> *"Get up, sir!" I cried, and he leaped to the floor,*
> *But my wife merely sighed, and said,*
> > *"Nevermore."*
> *"Who are you, foul creature?" I called to this man,*
> *With all vocal force that I could command.*
> *Embarrassed, he said, "My name it is Billy,*
> *And I just happened in for a bowl of your chili."*
> *When he said what he said, my hackles did rise,*
> *And I looked at this lout, dead in his eyes,*
> *And I said, "Let me tell you, you bastardly Billy,*
> *You may share my wife, but never my chili."*

This may be said of Eck Bludsoe's verse—his cadenced phrases evoke deep feelings at once archaic and humane. He

144

does his work without whiskers. We find something of the rhythms of Ossian in his parallelistic lines. His metrical unresistant freedom fits neatly into the pattern of Duncanville civilization, Dallas County. Finally, there is assonance here, especially in the first poem quoted.

An Associated Press dispatch out of Houston gave indication that the Terlingua dispute was having serious repercussions. In a Houston restaurant a customer named Thomas H. Raymond ordered a bowl of chili. When it came he ran his spoon through it and then summoned the manager, Willy Wilson. Mr. Raymond *complained that there were no beans in his chili.* The manager, Mr. Willy Wilson, asserted that there should never be beans in chili. The customer said the manager was insane, that chili without beans was not true chili. The argument grew hotter than the chili itself and Manager Wilson produced a gun and fired a bullet into the floor, at the same time ordering Thomas H. Raymond to get the hell out of his place. Mr. Raymond responded by picking up a beer bottle and clouting Mr. Wilson with it. Whereupon Mr. Wilson shot Mr. Raymond dead.

There should be beans in chili.

Another news item concerned with a happening in a Texas restaurant came out of San Antonio. It has nothing to do with chili but I think it is appropriate. At a San Antonio drive-in, Antonio Rojas ordered a hamburger. The waitress responded by accusing Rojas of bullying her brother; she pulled out a gun and shot Antonio. He slumped just a little and said, "Make that a hamburger to go." She brought it to him and he drove away eating it and clutching his wound, and took himself to Robert B. Green hospital.

The extent of the interest in The Confrontation was being amply illustrated at this time by a steady flow of long-distance calls to the Ponderosa. The callers for the most part were newspapers, seeking telephonic interviews with either Wick Fowler or me, and these came from San Francisco, Omaha, Chicago, Toledo, Pittsburgh, Miami, New Orleans, and from scores of papers all around Texas. There also were calls from well-wishers and radio stations and nuts. While Mr. Fowler was still resident in the motel he was so besieged by radio stations putting him on the air, via telephonic talk, that at one point he called out to me: "The highway patrol guys just stopped by and said they wanted to interview us on their radar."

Some of the phone calls for me came from far-off people offering suggestions about how I could defeat my opponent. These suggestions usually involved certain ingredients I was told to put in my chili. One man in El Paso urged me to use soy beans instead of pinto beans. He seemed fanatically eager for me to beat Fowler and there is an explanation for this; El Paso is so far away from all other parts of Texas, save the sparsely settled southwestern counties, that the town is oriented in the direction of New Mexico, which comes right up to the El Paso city limits. El Paso newspapers consistently feature New Mexico news rather than Texas news, and the people of El Paso entertain harsh opinions about Austin and Dallas and Fort Worth and Corpus and San Antonio. I think if a poll had been taken it would have shown a majority of El Paso citizens rooting for me. Notwithstanding this, I had to tell the helpful gentleman that I would never sully my chili with soy beans. "To be quite frank," I said, "any sensible person knows that God gave us soy beans to be pressed into paving bricks."

There were others who told me of a recently discovered trick of putting chocolate in chili. I was informed that David Witts, the Dallas lawyer who is Mayor of Terlingua, uses chocolate—one heaping tablespoon of powdered cocoa added to the pot is said to impart a rich coloring, a certain smoothness. I remembered then that Joe Cooper, the Prophet, made mention of chocolate in chili in The Bible. High Priest Cooper said that the chocolate serves to give the chili an easy consistency and a better coloring and could not be tasted itself. At this writing I have not tried it, and I hesitate to do so—it impresses me as being just one more bit of idiotic tampering on the part of undiscriminating Texans.

I have a copy of a letter I wrote years ago to Ira Smith, who collaborated with me on a couple of baseball books and who admired to make chili the way I made it. In this letter I gave Ira my recipe again, because he had lost it, and I concluded with: "The stuff gets better as the season wears on—you can eat offen it for a week. After the third day one of Honus Wagner's discarded jockstraps will pep it up." Makes as much sense to me as soy beans. No matter how much they roar and boast about hewing to the line, Texans overdo on ingredients; they can't avoid experimentation in making chili, or in making anything else, including money. During my recent bumming tours around the State I happened to hear about a hair tonic made in Dallas. Someone told me it was a good product. It is called Baker's, and the people who make it come right out and say, on the telly, that it is the best hair tonic in the world. I bought a bottle of it and one day happened to look at the label where the ingredients are listed. It said, "Essence of Cantharides." Spanish fly hair tonic! My god, people will be *drinking* it.

A letter came to me from Mrs. Kirby Kean of California with talk about *chiles rellenos* and other Mexican comes-

147

tibles and Mrs. Kean took me to task for using grocery-store chili powder as against hand-shredded raw chiles. In my answer I said:

> I wrote that *Holiday* piece for people who live in the North. You cannot ever tell a citizen of the Southwest, and especially a citizen of Texas, how to make chili. You cannot tell a Texan how to make anything. Northerners who don't know any better would never be able to find the stores where they could get real chiles, or the product of real chiles. It is easy for them to get chili powder, and I disagree with southwesterners who turn up their noses at that product. It is not all *that* inferior. It is possible to get good chili powder and make good chili with it. There is a Mexican store on Fourteenth Street in NYC where they sell chili powder in bulk—they grind it themselves—and it gives chili a fine flavor. Nuts to the Texas purists who say they cannot abide the stuff used by the common people. Any chili-maker with imagination and a genuine love of the stuff will eventually find his way to the best ingredients.

The phone jangled on as zero hour approached and I had to issue swift and concise public statements concerning my fitness and my feelings. I told one caller that I had just been informed that Wick Fowler uses liberal quantities of ground-up corncobs in his chili, calling it masa, and that I felt certain no jury in America would ever vote approval of corncob chili. I told a young man in San Angelo that as soon as I arrived in Terlingua I was bringing charges of castra-metation against the whole Dallas crowd. He repeated the word and didn't want to ask its meaning, didn't want to let on that he didn't know, and I could tell that he was suspicious of it. I told him to look it up. It means "making camp before battle."

Jim Glasscock, boss of the Alpine *Avalanche*, took me to call on W. D. Smithers, an important citizen of the Southwest. Mr. Smithers has been described by Dudley R. Dobie as "an expert photographer, a master engineer-mapmaker, a newspaper correspondent, an inventor, an artist, a naturalist, a soldier—and, most important, a well-read, extensively traveled, brilliant historian." Mr. Smithers talked at length about Terlingua and the Big Bend country and then I eased him into the subject of chili. He said that chili is a Texas invention, devised by lazy people.

"The Texans," said this Texan, "were too bone-lazy to make *mole*, which is Mexico's great contribution to cookery. *Mole*, when it is properly prepared, contains as many as twenty-seven ingredients and two and a half days are required to cook it. If you are going to have *mole* sauce for your turkey, you begin it on Monday morning. You cook and add ingredients night and day for two and a half days, and then about noon on Wednesday it is ready. Texans would never go to all that trouble. So they messed around, looking for something easier to make, and they came up with chili."

Mr. Smithers gave me a recipe for turkey *mole* as prepared by one of Mexico's leading gourmet cooks, Senora Donna Amalia Hernandez, the founder, director, and choreographer of Ballet Folklorico of Mexico. *Mole* is served traditionally with turkey, but it works with chicken too, and this is the way Senora Hernandez fabricates it:

TURKEY MOLE

Preheat deep fryer to 370 degrees. Cut up a 12- to 14-pound turkey. Dip pieces in milk, then flour, and dry on rack. Prepare six Chimayo peppers, six broad peppers, and three chile peppers. If they are dry, drop into hot water 10 minutes before removing seeds and veins. Preheat oven to 325 degrees. Deep-fry turkey pieces 5 minutes in pepper-flavored fat. Drain and place in large casserole. Cover with turkey or game stock. Cover dish and bake for 1 hour.

149

Toast in dry pan over gentle heat 1 tablespoon sesame seed, ½ cup pine nuts, ½ cup blanched almonds. Grind together 2 tortillas and the browned peppers.

Cook 3 minced garlic cloves in 2 tablespoons oil. Add 2 cups peeled, seeded tomatoes, 1 bay leaf, ½ teaspoon coriander, 3 cloves, 1 teaspoon cinnamon.

Combine the above ingredients with nuts and pepper mixture and simmer 15 minutes. Put this thick sauce with 2 cups of turkey stock over the cut-up turkey and simmer, covered, 2½ hours.

This dish may be made a day or two before serving, but just before serving add 2 ounces grated chocolate, mixing it well into the heated sauce.

Mr. Smithers said the Hernandez recipe is the quick method for preparing *mole* and he believes that the Senora rigged this recipe for lazy Texans.

SIXTEEN

Der Tag came, and the early sunlight dappled the mountains which surround the town of Alpine on all sides, presenting a splendid panorama of ever-changing hues, hour after hour. This can be said for Alpine: it owns as beautiful a setting as ever a man could ask for.

Judge Hallie Stillwell arrived at the Ponderosa before eight o'clock, bringing my hawg-leg, an old .45 six-shooter that she borrowed from Tom Leary of Marathon. Tom is the rancher we met on the Cloralex fishing expedition on the Rio Grande. Judge Stillwell explained about the hawg-leg; it was once the personal weapon of Tom Leary's uncle, Clyde Buttrill, who was a Texas Ranger and who farred this selfsame six-shooter many's the time at Mescans who rode with Pancho Villa. I put the gun and belt in my briefcase where I had already packed my groceries, including the secret ingredients. Sue and Leo Thomason, who run the Ponderosa restaurant, waved us good-bye as we drove away. We headed south from Alpine and about five miles out I thought I saw Maury Maverick and Frank Tolbert skulking behind a clump of claret-cup cactus near the highway. Claret-cup cactus grows to a height of fourteen inches. I could not figure out any kind of an ambush they may have been planning, so I assumed they had been shooting craps.

Someone in Alpine told me that Tolbert owns a pair of dice that have a peculiar tendency to *lean* before they settle into place; they seem to flop over in slow motion, the way it was told to me. We sped along our way.

Hallie Stillwell talked about her early days in Brewster County and some of her experiences as a schoolteacher in Presidio where, from time to time, she had to ring the bell and dismiss the kids on account of Pancho Villa and his cutthroats arriving in town. She explained all about the evil screwworm and how it has finally been conquered—the greatest single progressive development in cattle ranching, she said, in a hundred years. She remembered how her husband and other ranchers used to snicker at the college perfessers who concerned themselves with animal husbandry and the study of grasses and so on. "And so," said Hallie, "it turned out that the perfessers solved this big problem by simply dropping boxes of sterile screwworm flies out of airplanes."

Back where I come from people think of all Texas as being like a tortilla, flat. They don't know about the towering mountains of Southwest Texas. The town of Alpine sets at 4,484 feet above sea level and is surrounded by peaks that rise higher than 7,000 feet. The mountains of the Big Bend area, where Terlingua is located, are even more impressive. The gorgeous peaks appear to rise from the plain, dotted with Spanish dagger, the straight and stalwart yucca, the graceful and radiant ocotilla, and the white clouds drift overhead letting the sunlight dapple the mountain slopes in polychromatic shadings that . . . shet the cabin door, Nellie, they's a herd uh Hereford heifers a-comin' through the gate!

I must mention, too, the highways throughout West Texas —to the mind of a New Yorker they border on the supernatural for they are pool-table smooth and straight and wide and expertly engineered and they cover this vast territory in a comprehensive network, and they actually astonish an easterner by their lack of traffic; the motorist drives for hours on beautiful highway and seldom sees another vehicle.

We came in sight of Santiago Peak which rises ostensibly out of flat desertland to a height of 6,500 feet. Here we were, speeding toward Rio Grande country and the greatest incident of desert warfare since the defeat of Rommel in North Africa, and our talk was of Santiago Peak.

I became interested in this mountain during one of my previous visits to Brewster County. The peak rises in classic grandeur, as if it had started out with the intention of becoming a mountain of perfect proportions and then, perhaps two-thirds of the way up, it is sheared off. This leaves an immense flat plain at the top, and it was on this broad mesa that Progress City was founded. I did a lot of traveling around the county trying to gather facts about Progress City but the people of Brewster, who ordinarily will talk a leg off of you, clammed up on this particular subject. The story of Progress City is a story of a great and fantastic land swindle and I wanted to write about it for a national magazine, and had an assignment to do so, but the old folks who might have remembered the scandalous events of around 1910 wouldn't talk. I figured for a long time that it was a shame, that they were embarrassed because their homeland had been the setting for such an ignominious piece of business; that they were embarrassed by the fact that Alpine stands as one of the most prominent communities in the nation when it comes to real estate fraud. But I could have been wrong about their shame and embarrassment. Gage Holland, a Texan in the classic mold, big and handsome and easygoing, is a member of a family that owns, in Brewster County, three and a half acres more than the total area of Rhode Island. I appproached Mr. Holland and asked him why the old residents were reluctant to talk to me on the subject of Progress City. I said it didn't seem reasonable to me that Alpine should be all *that* ashamed of something that happened sixty years ago. "They're not ashamed," drawled Rancher Holland. "You got to understand one thing about this part of the country. The reason they don't tell you anything is they don't know anything. People around here got no sense to begin with, else they wouldn't be around here tryin' to make a livin'."

In the courthouse in Alpine the records of the swindle are solid and substantial, in plats and in hundreds of warranty deeds—so many of them that a special book, weighing more than a bull calf, is needed to contain them all.

Back about 1909 a man named Lee R. Davis came to Alpine and bought the level top of Santiago Peak. He then had the town of Progress City platted into 438 blocks, and each of these blocks was divided into 24 lots, or homesites. Ten thousand five hundred and twelve lots, halfway to heaven. And it's my impression that Mr. Lee R. Davis sold every one of them. I wasn't able to find out what he charged his suckers per lot—apparently he kept that a secret between himself and his God—but the record of the warranty deeds indicates that the sales were made, for the most part, in other sections of Texas. Some people say that Lee R. Davis did his slickering in New York City, but that isn't true. He was a patriotic Texan and he let his fellow Texans get in on his good thing. One fact about Progress City not known to the average citizen of Brewster County is the existence of a railroad in the community. Mr. Davis had a railroad running right through the middle of his town—it is clearly indicated on the plat—the Mexico, Kansas City & Orient Railroad, with a depot located right in the center of town. Whenever I think of Progress City, way the hell and gone up on top of that mountain—so far removed from the plain that it would shatter the cool of a burro who tried to get up there—I think of those railroad tracks, and I think too of Travis Roberts, who lives on a ranch near Marathon and whom I visited when I was seeking information. Mr. Roberts told me that very few human beings have ever made it to the top of Santiago and when I asked him what grew up there, he said, "If that land's got one jackrabbit on it, it's mighty overstocked."

The story goes that after Mr. Davis had sold off most of his high-rise lots, people began traveling to Alpine and Marathon with the intention of visiting their property and maybe drawing up plans for a bungalow. When this flow of victims into the area became a flood, the government of Brewster County apparently decided something ought to be done. It may be legend, but I was told that Mr. Lee R. Davis was located and fetched to Alpine and cross-examined. He seemed genuinely surprised that his honesty should be questioned. He said he hadn't ever told his customers that the land was on top of a mountain, but neither had he told them it was on a riverbank, or on a prairie. He hadn't lied to them. So the Commissioners puzzled over the matter and then asked Mr. Davis if he had staked out the property on the mountain. He said he had not. So the Commissioners told him to get his miserable ass up there and stake it, or they would put him in prison for life, and he had to do it, this poor honest nonlying man had to struggle up Santiago Peak with burros and wooden stakes and hammers and so on, and I imagine there were moments when he wished he'd never heard of Progress City or the Mexico, Kansas City & Orient Railroad, or Alpine, or Texas, for that matter.

Only two or three Alpine citizens fell for Mr. Davis and his fraud and bought lots. One of these, a local businessman, was a Davis victim and for the rest of his life was the butt of much kidding for his gullibility. He returned one day from a trip down below Santiago Peak and someone asked him: "Hey, Herbert, while you was down there did you visit your property?" And the businessman replied: "Nawp, but I leaned against it."

Realestateagentwise, as I may have hinted, Alpine appears to have an unusual and splotchy history. So does Texas. So does the United States. So does the world. A character in Edna Ferber's novel, *Giant*, comes upon some old books in a Texas ranch house and, in the words of Miss Ferber:

> The books turned out to be gnawed-looking volumes on Spanish land grants in Texas. Intended as a baldly stated record of early land transactions in the region, they actually were, quite consciously, a cloak-and-dagger account of such skullduggery, adventure, and acquisitive ruthlessness as to make the reader reject the whole as mythical. Settlers, pioneers, frontiersmen used cupidity against ignorance, turned land into cash and live men into dead men with blithe ferocity.

I am tempted to say that, since conditions haven't changed, the Texans of today have honorable precedent to guide them in their gay sport of thimblerigging the dudes. But Edna Ferber's testimony is of no value . . . in Texas. Whenever I have brought her name up among Texans they just shake their heads from side to side in a sort of dumb disbelief. I brought her in with the above excerpt just to show that all land fraud has not been concentrated in Alpine, though there is some evidence to the contrary.

In one of Botkin's folklore books there is a chapter out of *Bill Jones of Paradise*, an old-timey book by a man named Callison, detailing a journey from El Paso to San Antonio. The traveler arrives at Alpine and says, right off:

> I met one of the most crooked real estate agents in Alpine I ever saw in my life. He was so crooked that he could not sleep in a fence corner. He was so crooked that you could not tell by his tracks which way he was going. He had a barrel of snakes beat a country block. You could not tell by his city plot whether you were trying to buy a lot in

156

Alpine or in a prairie dog town four miles out. He dug a well that was so crooked that the water ran out at both ends. . . . He was so crooked that he had to put his hat on with a monkey wrench. . . . You can locate in Alpine if you wish to, but life is too short to stay there over a week. . . . After a few days spent in this magic city I went to San Antonio.

I would be inclined to put all this testimony down as ancient history and idle talk, except for the fact that just recently I ran across an item in a magazine describing a land fraud. The story concerned a man named Elvyn Eugene Boggs. Working around fairs and other public functions, Mr. Boggs defrauded the public out of about $60,000, according to the Post Office Department, by offering "free" lots, the recipient merely having to pay "closing costs." Actually, said the federal agency, the lots were in rocky and inaccessible land and were worth even less than those closing costs. Boggs got two years in prison. The story said he was from Alpine, Texas.

Running it all over in my mind I decided that if I ever had any occasion to do business with anybody in Alpine, I would exercise caution, and hire three lawyers, and pack a rod. Especially any business having to do with land.

Subsequently, however, I relaxed my vigilance because people told me that in Alpine there is no dishonesty, nobody ever locks the doors of his house, deceit is never practiced in advertising, that every human being in the town and some of the dogs go to church every Sunday and that, in the tradition of the Old West, in Alpine a man's word is his bond . . . and a handshake is as good as any written contract on earth. Merde.

SEVENTEEN

Terlingua is at once bleak and majestic. We drove into the ghost town around 10 o'clock in the morning and found about two dozen visitors already loafing about in the vicinity of the Terlingua Inn. This was a ramshackle 'dobe structure with a galvanized iron roof and a crumbling front porch, also covered with a metal roof. On this veranda two Coleman stoves had been set up—two burners set about a foot off the worn brick floor and connected with a tank of bottled gas. This was where the contestants were to cook.

The town itself consisted of the shells of perhaps fifty adobe houses, most of them just fragments of old walls. Next to the Terlingua Inn stood the adobe walls of the former Terlingua Opera House, which I explored briefly. A portion of the stage was still intact and all four walls were standing, but there was no roof. I counted it a great blessing that no one, all day long, told me that Sarah Bernhardt or Lily Langtry or Adelina Patti performed on that stage.

Someone had lettered handsome signs and posted them all over the immediate area of the Terlingua Inn. On the porch itself was the largest banner of all, proclaiming:

WELCOME H. ALLEN SMITH
IF THE YANKEES CAN STAND YOU, WE CAN

Someone said the signs were contributed by the smart ellick, Sam Huddleston. I copied down a few of them in my notebook, as follows:

THE BARTENDER DRINKS ONLY ON TWO
OCCASIONS
WHEN HE'S HAD CHILI FOR
BREAKFAST AND WHEN HE AIN'T

THE ONLY DIFFERENCE BETWEEN TERLINGUA
AND DALLAS
IS THAT DALLAS IS TALLER

ALL THIS COUNTRY NEEDS TO MAKE IT
LIVABLE IS WATER
COME TO THINK ABOUT IT,
THAT'S ALL HELL NEEDS

WHEN THE GOOD LORD SENT THE FLOOD
ALL WE GOT WAS A QUARTER OF AN INCH

GOAT-HERDERS, LIGHTNIN' ROD SALESMEN,
NEWSPAPER WRITERS
AND OTHER SUCHLIKE
KINELY USE THE BACK DOOR

NEXT TIME TWO HOURS HANGS HEAVY
ON YOUR HANDS, SPEND IT ON OUR
FRONT PORCH. ALONG IN THE COOL OF
THE EVENING WE PRESENT: "SUNSET
OVER THE CHISOS" IN NATURAL COLOR
AND ON THE WIDEST SCREEN ON EARTH.
. . . IT'S PURE BEAUTY GONE PLUMB
LOCO IN THIN BLUE AIR. ALL PROPS TEN
TIMES OLDER THAN THE PYRAMIDS. ALL
SUNSETS PAINTED PERSONALLY BY THE
LORD.

I can't quite understand why this wild stretch of country leads people to thinking about Eternity and God and all. In the same spirit in which Mark Twain's "prose poem" is always quoted about the Hawaiian Islands, so it is that Ludwig Bemelmans is quoted about his visit to the Big Bend country. In 1956 Mr. Bemelmans wrote in *McCall's*:

> Leaving Highway 90 at Marathon, we came to the Big Bend country toward sunset, that part of Texas where the Rio Grande makes a U-shaped bend in its course. In a lifetime spent in traveling, here I came upon the greatest wonder. The mantle of God touches you; it is panorama without beginning or end. No fire can burn so bright, no projection can duplicate the colors that dance over the desert or the bare rock formations that form the backdrop. No words can tell you, and no painter hold it. It is only to be visited and looked at with awe. It will make you breathe deeply whenever you think of it, for you have inhaled eternity.

It is my judgment that Mr. Bemelmans was a trifle stoned when he composed that paean.

Once I was on the scene, things began to come a little more into focus. The land where Terlingua stands is owned jointly by David A. Witts, the Dallas lawyer, and Carroll Shelby, a swashbuckling racing driver from Los Angeles, who is responsible for, among other things, the Ford sports car called the Shelby Cobra. These two men also have their 220,000-acre ranch twenty or thirty miles to the north of Terlingua on the road to Alpine. The ranch has been named, at various times, the Christmas Mountains Ranch, the White Windmill, the Witts–Shelby, the Chiricahua, the White Arrow, and, most recently, the Terlingua Ranch.

The ghost town of Terlingua itself has been a plaything of the Dallas Chili Appreciation Society. Lawyer Witts, as has been noted, is the Mayor and there is a long list of additional city officials. I cite a few:

Water Commissioner, Frank X. Tolbert.
City Meteorologist, James Underwood.
Terlingua Airport Manager, George Haddaway.
Social Director, Carroll Shelby.
Chief Justice, Municipal Court, Thomas J. Tierney.
Chief Chili-Head, Wick Fowler.
Director, Museum of Modern Art (actually the ladies' outdoor privy), B. R. Neale.
Director of Libraries, Holland McCombs. (The only book permitted in the Terlingua Public Library is *A Bowl of Red*, by Tolbert. Otherwise, the library is a sagging *al fresco* outhouse, a two-holer.)
City Secretary, Buck Marryat. (Mr. Marryat is also chief fire-starter for Wick Fowler.)
Director, Sanitation Department Band, Irving Harrigan.
Inspector of Hides, Ben Atwell.
Captain of the Port of Terlingua, Alfred C. Anderson.
Director of Weights and Measures, Keith Shelton.
Editor, The Terlingua *Tarantula*, Paul Crume.
Keeper of the General Store, Fred Swartz.

When news of the closely knit nature of Terlingua's government got around the United States there were some unusual reactions. A man named Manning, living in El Paso, wrote a letter demanding that he be given some official position because he is, so far as he knows, the only living native of Terlingua. In a letter to me he enclosed a certified copy of his birth certificate and he asked several questions. Were rental cars available in Terlingua? Was the Terlingua-Hilton accessible to the contest grounds? After remarking that he has a Jewish friend who makes kosher chili, Mr. Manning asked: "If my friend is eligible to enter the contest, can you tell us where we may obtain a circumcized goat?"

I wrote this Mr. Manning, addressing him as an obvious impostor and advising him that if he hopes to muscle into the Terlingua picture he had best hasten. I said:

> Mayor Witts has just informed me that he is instituting proceedings looking toward the secession of Terlingua from the Union. It will become, under this scheme, a separate and independent nation. I have already applied for the job of King and I think I'll get it. If I become King of Terlingua I'll make it hot for pretenders and impostors and bureaucrats alike. Also women. I've always had a feeling that Kinging would come natural to me. I'm built for it, and got the right kind of head.
>
> H. Allen Smith, Rex.

Another letter came from Carter Jenkins, of Springfield, Illinois, applying for the post of city engineer of Terlingua. Mr. Jenkins furnished a long list of qualifications, the most consonant of which was: "My work in the engineering profession began at the age of twelve when I was water boy with a survey crew for the Memphis, Dallas & Gulf Railroad which, unfortunately, never reached Memphis, Dallas or the Gulf."

Over the weeks preliminary to The Confrontation many pretty things were written about Terlingua. Nat Henderson, for example, composed a touching panegyric in which he said that the leaves would turn russet in the autumn air if there were any leaves. Someone else, calling attention to the majestic aspects of the Big Bend scenery, said that Terlingua is the fartherest you can go without getting anywhere. Terlingua was selected for the chili contest, reported Harley Pershing, because it was the only place on earth where a disaster would never be noticed, the town itself being a disaster. The official stationery of the town government proclaims the fact that when LBJ declared war on poverty, Terlingua promptly wanted to know where to surrender.

162

I must make some mention of the heroic redmen who were well-known to the Big Bend Country in former times. This was the stamping ground of the noble Comanche. The great Comanche trail came down from Fort Stockton to Marathon and on southward to the Rio Grande. It was the whim of these Indians to ride periodically down this trail, plundering and killing all along the way, and then go into Mexico and loot whole towns, raping and robbing and burning, usually to get a few horses. It was their way of doing business. These gentle nomadic redskins had wants that were simple. They knew not good chili, or chili of any kind. They ate the succulent prickly pear, picking their teeth with the thorns, and they took piñon nuts and beat them into mush and rolled the mush into balls and ate the balls along the frolicsome trail.

It must have been exciting and stimulating to watch a group of the Comanches moving down the trail which today is the highway to Hallie Stillwell's ranch and the mining village of La Linda. The Comanche men wore loose-fitting cloaks of mangy buffalo hide and ugly leggings of deerskin grown as stiff as corrugated iron. When I was a kid I sometimes read about how the Indians made their clothing from deerskin and other wilderness leathers, and I always imagined that their materials were as soft and pliable as satin. Not so. Those Comanche boys wore leather flaps over their whammadoodles and this leather turned so stiff and unyielding with the passage of time that the wearer had to be careful sitting down, or even walking, lest he emasculate himself.

According to Carl Raht, historian of the Big Bend and the Davis Mountains, the men were "usually squat of stature and crooked of limb." The women, on the other hand, were small and mean-looking; a man stepping off a whaling vessel after seven years at sea would have hesitated—would likely have covered his eyes and shuddered and said I'll wait. One of the reasons for his shuddering could have been the condition of the noses on many of the Comanche women. When a Comanche squaw was caught poontanging around with some smelly buck other than her husband, her nose was cut off. This gave her a peculiar look. A woman whose nose has been cut off by an angry Comanche husband, using a stone hunting knife, is not likely to win even a second at Atlantic City.

EIGHTEEN

More and more cars were coming down the soda-ash road to Terlingua. Wick Fowler arrived, got out of his vehicle, put on a Mexican straw hat bigger around than a wagon wheel, tied on his Dallas chili bib, and told me he was sick. Virus, he said. Then he began describing the proceedings at the Witts–Shelby ranch where the Dallas people and their friends had spent the night in carouse. Mr. Fowler said that most of the men at the ranch *tried* to get some sleep but there was a noisy poker game in progress all night and an intoxicated cowboy lovingly known as Tooter insisted on riding his horse and screeching yippees indoors and out. Harold Wynne, the manager of the ranch, told Mr. Fowler that he was equipped to sleep sixteen in comparative comfort, and for this epochal night he had to provide for 268 guests. It was reported that Mr. Wynne and his wife, along about 2 o'clock in the morning, entered into a suicide pact but they were kept so busy that they never got to carry it out.

"Those among us," said Mr. Fowler, "who wanted to get some sleep took our gear into this big basement storeroom. Got into our bedrolls and sleeping bags and got the lights turned off. Then someone crept up, opened a big door, drove a herd of goats inside, slammed the door shut, and slapped a

165

padlock on it. I can't remember any worse pandemonium anywhere in the half-dozen wars I have covered."

Quite a few members of the Dallas cabal chose to spread their bedding on the ground outside the stone ranch house, but they were unable to sleep because of Cowboy Tooter, who invented a little game in which he rode back and forth jumping his horse over the reclining Texans. Some of them said, with bitterness, that the Big Bend Country was the sorriest piece of country they had ever laid eyes on.

A bus came chugging into the Terlingua compound and a good portion of the aristocratic membership of the Chili Appreciation Society International began unloading. They were unshaven, red-eyed, and trying hard not to be sullen and grumpy. It may have been imagination, but my nostrils picked up goat-smell. These men filed as rapidly as they could into the main lobby of the Terlingua Inn—the main lobby being the sum total of the edifice—where I got the impression someone was dispensing booze and beer. Ere long the whoreson beetle-heads from Dallas began to show signs of feeling better. There was much intramural goosing. After a while an amplifying system was hooked up at the opposite end of the long veranda from the cooking area, and Bill Rives, a newspaper editor from Denton, Texas, assumed charge, summoning all of the principals to the microphone. Mr. Rives said that there would be, at this time, some opening ceremonies and I murmured to myself, "Good God, don't tell me they're gonna open with prayer." I have already mentioned that everything is opened with prayer in Texas— City Council meetings, poker games, the showing of stag movies.

Mr. Rives of Denton faced the people and spoke. "We will open these proceedings," he said, "with prayer. The chili prayer."

He summoned Maury Maverick to the mike and Mr. Maverick spoke the prayer which is attributed to an old-time

166

Negro range cook named Bones Hooks. Bones recited his chili prayer extemporaneously at a cowboy reunion in Amarillo, and it goes thisaway:

Lord God, you know us old cowhands is forgetful. Sometimes, I cain't even recollect what happened yestiddy. We *is* forgetful. We just know daylight and dark, summer, fall, winter, and sprang. But I sure hope we don't never forget to thank you before we eat a mess of good chili.

We don't know why, in your wisdom, you been so doggone good to us. The heathen Chinee don't have no chili, never. The Frenchmans is left out. The Rooshians don't know no more about chili than a hawg knows about a sidesaddle. Even the Mescans don't get a good whiff of chili less they live around here.

Chili-eaters is some of your chosen people, Lord. We don't know why you so doggone good to us. But Lord, God, don't never think we ain't grateful for this chili we about to eat. Amen.

Mr. Rives now instructed the Fort Stockton musicians to play "Hello Dolly" while he led the assemblage in the town's official anthem, "Hello Terlingua," a number composed by Mr. Rives himself. It was godawful from any and all points of view. After that he tried to present me with an impressive document which would make me, by dispensation of the Governor, an honorary citizen of Texas. I rejected it brusquely, declaring that I entertained no plan to behave in any honorable way during my stay in Texas.

Mr. Fowler was called to the mike and announced that he had been asked to cook extra chili to be mixed into the water supply of Terlingua and into the ship channel down at Pasadena, Texas. Terlingua wanted Fowler chili dumped into its principal body of water, Dirty Woman Creek, instead of fluoride, so that citizens of the town would have fewer cavities. "It is a sure thing," said Mr. Fowler, "that they will have fewer cavities than any other place on earth, because they have fewer teeth." He said that Dick Nichols of the Pasadena *News-Citizen* had asked for a tablespoon of Fowler chili to drop into the ship channel for the purpose of neutralizing pollution all the way up to Houston. Mr. Fowler also announced that he had just received a stern warning from the Food and Drug Administration that he had to label his chili as "habit-forming."

Now came the signal to begin, the thumps on the copper washboiler, the gas burners were lighted by Harley Pershing and Buck Marryat with more flourishes than characterize the opening of the Olympic Games, and the *guerre à mort* was on.

We cooked at a distance of six feet from each other and from the beginning Mr. Fowler comported himself in a manner aimed at endearing himself to the crowd; his friends excused his conduct, saying that he had years of close association with the politicians of Austin. We cooked under trying circumstances. For two hours I had to work at my chili with one hand and fight off tourists with the other—travelers who had come over from the scenic areas of Big Bend National Park and who seemed eager to snatch the lid off my pot and taste my incomparable chili. The average American tourist is a predatory souvenir-grabber and has to be watched, and sometimes frisked. I have been closely observant of tourists for many years, having made it my business to study them at their play. There on that porch at Terlingua there were ladies who boldly shoved me aside, lifted the lid off my pot, seized spoons, and dipped. In every case I just as roughly shoved *them* aside and cussed them a bit. They were in quest of a strange and intangible something—the right to brag, when they got home, that down their miserable gullets had gurgled a whole blamed spoonful of championship chili. They knew that the chili contest was being publicized and talked about throughout the land, and this was a special touristic achievement, gobbling chili at Terlingua.

By now the whole dusty area before the Inn was alive with people and my wife, who kept moving around and talking to the visitors, told me later that it was one of the greatest and most colorful spectacles she had ever witnessed, being part Mexican fiesta, part Fourth of July picnic, part Indian rain dance, and part political rally (there were several congressmen and members of the Texas Legislature present, plus a small army of law enforcement officers under the direction of Sheriff Carl Williams of Brewster County). My wife said there was an *unreal* quality to the spectacle, and she had a feeling that she was on location with a movie company. She also whispered to me, "I do believe there is some drinking going on." Yet only one shot was fired during the whole affair; the sound of it came from somewhere out back and the fast gun was never identified, though someone said it was a man shooting at the Terlingua Museum of Modern Art. And there were only three fist fights all day long. One was over a woman, one involved the superiority of Colorado pinto beans over the Texas variety, and one was over beans period.

From time to time evidence arose that there were plots, subplots, and counterplots afoot, involving the promotion of (a) a proposed resort hotel for Terlingua; (b) a brand of beer; (c) another brand of beer; (d) a brand of whisky; (e) a brand of chili; (f) books, and (g) an automobile racing course. There were some who said that I was involved in the affair for the sole purpose of promoting a book of mine that was then on the market. No such thing. Few Texans ever crack a book—a fact well-known to the publishing industry —unless it is a book written by Ruth Montgomery or Emmet Fox.

At one point in the tournament a woman came up to me bearing a huge floral piece. She said she was a tourist from

Missouri and that she had stopped in a florist shop in the town of Marfa tu ask directions. They were just finishing up the floral horseshoe, composed of red and white carnations interlaced with bright red chiles, and they asked the Missouri lady if she would deliver it to me at Terlingua. The Missouri lady was rather vague about the assignment, possibly because the ribbon on the horseshoe stated boldly: "Chili Champion H. Allen Smith From Holiday Magazine." I was too busy cooking to be bothered by this premature tribute and I asked the Missouri lady to take it inside the Inn and stand it against a wall somewhere. Before she departed with it she said to me:

"This thing cost a heap. I spose you're gettin' a kickback on it."

At that precise moment I had a feeling that the intrinsic theme of The Great Chili Confrontation had been pinpointed, crystallized, by the words of that nice old lady from Missouri.

I mixed and added ingredients and stirred and watched the predatory tourists and listened to the solemn comments of the ranchers who stood back of the ropes near me and studied my every movement. I also kept an eye on Wick Fowler, analyzing his culinary style, best described as Early Truck Stop.

Before he ever started, before he put a single ingredient in his pot, he walked past it quickly . . . for suet.

Later I overheard him in conversation with a lady journalist. "Madam," he said, "I'll have you know I am more than just a chili expert; I have been, for seventeen years, first violinist with the Falfurrias Symphony." The man was already building his alibi. And I heard him ask Art Leibson of the El Paso *Times* about the size of the crowd. Leibson said he figured about two thousand. "Well," said Mr. Fowler, frowning in concentration, "lemme see now . . . there's twenty-three hundred in a thousand, so that makes . . ." I felt that he was tiring.

Two days earlier a rule had been announced under which nobody would be allowed on the porch except the contestants, the judges, the musicians, and privileged members of the Chili Appreciation Society (meaning the total membership). Now that the cooking was actually under way, the porch was a caterwauling madhouse. Mr. Fowler and I were steadily besieged by young men bearing microphones and asking for comments on cookery in general, on mod styles, on Texas politics, on national politics, on the war in Vietnam, on everything. I remember that Mr. Fowler told them he had been in Vietnam as a correspondent for a Texas newspaper.

"While I was over there," he said, "I always spoke Spanish to the Vietnamese."

"How come?"

"Because it's a lot easier for them to learn Spanish than it is for me to learn Vietnamese."

For a television crew I heard Mr. Fowler speak glowingly of "the wonderful urban renewal projects LBJ has put into effect here in Terlingua"—an LBJ joke committed in a land where the LBJ joke burgeons and proliferates like lechuguilla, greasewood, and the wild wild hog.

They asked me why I didn't have a hired hand to stand by and skim the scum off the top of my chili, the way Wick Fowler was doing it. The Texans perform this rite all the time and call it "skinning off the fat." I asserted that "no Illinois Smith ever scam the scum off of his chili," that it was against the religious beliefs of Illinois Smiths to commit such an act.

Jean Glasscock, columnist for the Alpine *Avalanche,**

* Thirty miles to the east of Alpine there was once a weekly newspaper called the Marathon *Hustler.*

171

came by to wish me well and I put her to work. I asked her to circle around and get a taste of Mr. Fowler's cuckleburr chowder. She came back and said that the Fowler chili was taking on a greenish-yellow coloration and tasted of bean curd and soy sauce. Half an hour later I noticed that Mr. Fowler was shoveling more guck into his pot, and I sent out my spy again. This time she said she thought she detected fragments of wood, little splinters, in the Fowler chili and that it had a taste that put her in mind of shellac and swamp water. "I do believe," said Mrs. Glasscock, "that he is making pecky-cypress chili." She also said that Mr. Fowler's stuff was real fiery, suggesting that I might want to heat mine up a trifle. I dug into my supplies and came up with a few *chilipiquin* peppers which have been described conservatively: "They make chili so hot it will boil on a cold stove, and it will rest on your stomach like a litter of angry wildcats." I dropped four of these into my pot, for authority.

There were times when I was called away from my cooking, to meet celebrated guests, to participate in the taping of TV shows on the far side of the porch, and to speak to the crowd over the amplifying system. The populace seemed to be predominantly female and many of the women were hostile toward me. They were churn-butted females, for the most part, and faulty at the other end as well. There were moments when they were heckling me when I thought of Edna Ferber's line in *Giant:* ". . . the high shrill voices of Texas women."

I noted the arrival of another busload of Dallas derelicts from the ranch. This consignment included the two enemy judges and a man who staggered off the bus hollering a four-letter word. Some others among the newcomers said the bus had hit two mountain lions on its way down from the ranch; ten minutes later the number of mountain lions hit had been increased to six, plus three coyotes, an antelope, and a pair of savage javelinas. One passenger swore that the bus had been dive-bombed by a squadron of bald eagles. While I was away from my pot getting this news, Art Leibson of El Paso came charging up and said the tourists were fooling with my chili again; he said these were tourists obviously in the hire of the Dallas crowd, and he had observed one of them putting something that looked like grasshopper legs into my pot. "The thigh parts," said Mr. Leibson.

The moment had come. I got out the gun of Tom Leary's uncle and strapped it on and glared at the spectators.

David Witts came onto the platform accompanied by Floyd Schneider. This Schneider, a hired gun, had been pressed into service as a judge, replacing Maury Maverick, Jr. Mr. Maverick had been canned for the reason that his political philosophy was not clear to the Dallasites. I was curious about this new guy and looked him up and down carefully. He was a specimen that anthropologists would have rejected. Both he and David Witts were unshaven and bleary-eyed after what must have been a night of sin at the ranch. From their general appearance I surmised that they had been sniffing quite a bit of airplane glue. They were in no condition to judge skimmed milk, or a tarantula race.

On the other hand Hallie Stillwell was clear-eyed and alert. And clean-shaven.

NINETEEN

It was a noisy affair. There was whooping and yelling across the flats, and a banging of fenders as more and more automobiles arrived. Some thoughtful member of the organizing staff had trucked in six Japanese motorbikes on the theory that members of the press could use them to rush their dispatches and their film back to the landing strip some distance up the highway.

Members of the press decided that they were having too much fun in Terlingua to waste time in such journalistic derring-do. Yet they wanted to ride those Japanese bikes.

I never heard greater traffic noises in Times Square, or in the Place de la Concorde, than were elicited now in Terlingua. The picaresque knights of newspaperdom employed the bikes in open warfare, charging into one another and ramming their machines headlong into parked cars. I heard that a San Antonio political writer drove one of the bikes head-on into an automobile, was thrown over the handlebars and onto the hood, striking the slanted windshield which zoomed him upward and over in a fine parabola and landed him several feet to the rear of the car. He struggled to his feet, shook off some of the white dust, and predicted that Preston Smith would be the next governor of Texas. His flight sobered the other cyclists a trifle and they took their machines into a nearby alkali prairie and organized a game of polo, playing with rocks.

While the motorcycle shenanigans were in progress a leading rancher of the neighborhood, Rex Ivey of La Jitas, drove into the grounds. Mr. Ivey is a weather prophet of some renown. He stands on the north bank of the Rio Grande and gazes across to *el otra lado,* the other side, where he observes the rain dances of the Indians. He then calculates the weather for the whole of Brewster County and phones this information up to Judge Hallie Stillwell in Alpine, and Judge Stillwell puts it in her column in the Alpine *Avalanche* and everybody says, "Move th' stock inta th' cottonwood pasture and fetch th' summer furniture inta th' house . . . Rex Ivey's Indinns say it's gonna stawm." Mr. Ivey is, in addition, a member of the Brewster County Board of Commissioners. As he arrived on the Terlingua scene one of the fist fights was in progress, the one about pinto beans from Colorado. Mr. Ivey was observing the fight as he walked along, and he collided with an old lady who looked a good deal like Whistler's Mother. The little old lady called him four obscene names before ever he could blurt out an apology.

"I was shook," said Mr. Ivey. He climbed back into his car and drove swiftly to the river, and gazed across to *el otra lado,* hoping for the serenity of rain dances and revolutions.

About this time a distinguished-looking couple approached me—distinguished by the fact that they were neatly dressed and looked as if they had bathed and were not sweating quarts like everyone else. The gentleman, who wore modified western attire and resembled the Jack Holt of yesteryear, introduced himself as Ed Bartholomew. He was from Fort Davis, a historic community north of Alpine. He is a publisher of books concerned with western history and he writes some of the books he publishes.

"If," he said, "it would appear that I am skulking a little,

175

and appear to be nervous, it's just that I get that way now-adays when I'm around crowds of people with big hats on. Wyatt Earp is responsible."

I sought elucidation, of course, and he furnished it. He had become aggravated when he read a biography in which Wyatt Earp was canonized and made into a great and heroic character. Mr. Bartholomew went to work. He traveled all over the West, digging into old newspaper files and regional historic works. Eventually he wrote two fat books, *Wyatt Earp: The Untold Story*, and *Wyatt Earp: The Man & The Myth*. He demonstrated that the dashing hero of movies and television and many ignorant-type writers was no hero. He was never Marshal of anything, except for a period when he served as Town Marshal of Lamar, Missouri. He was never Marshal in Dodge City, in Wichita, in Tombstone, or in any of the other lawless towns of the Old West. He had served as a policeman in Wichita and Dodge City, according to Mr. Bartholomew's researches, and his main job was to keep the fire barrels at the street corners full of water and to collect shakedown money from the whorehouses.

Wyatt Earp, said Mr. Bartholomew, was arrested more times himself than he ever arrested others. He stole horses from Indians in Oklahoma Territory, was arrested and taken in chains to Fort Smith; he was a pimp, a thief, a dealer in bribes, a bail-jumper, and his girl friends were almost always prostitutes.

"The record shows," said Mr. Bartholomew, "that Earp actually did shoot one man in his career—himself. In Wichita he went to sleep in a chair that was tilted against a wall. The chair slipped and fell, and Wyatt's gun went off and shot him in the butt. Thereafter he was nicknamed Rump-shot Earp in Wichita and that may be one reason he left town."

Mr. Bartholomew put all this information into his books,

plus much more, and a large portion of the West rose up against him. He was warned that he would be strung up if he ever got near Tombstone where the name of Wyatt Earp is revered; he was told that he would be lynched in Wichita, and in Dodge. Newspaper editors in the cowtowns railed against him and called him a boob. Wherefore Mr. Bartholomew's apprehension around crowds of men wearing big hats.

I told him that I felt a strong literary kinship with him for once I branded the American saint, Will Rogers, a phoney and a fraud and a liar, in print. There were demands that my American citizenship be taken away from me, there were published suggestions that I be garroted at some public spot in Claremore, Oklahoma. I still say that Will Rogers was a mountebank, and Mr. Bartholomew continues to contend that Wyatt Earp was an effervescent nudnick.

When he had finished telling me about Wyatt Earp, his wife, Sophia, interjected a fascinating thought into the Terlingua scene. She said that she had been reading various newspaper accounts of the cooking contest and that it was often called "the chili war."

"Just suppose," said Mrs. Bartholomew, "that the news reached some of those Arab countries in the Near East. News that a bitter chili war has broken out in the southwestern part of the United States. Those Arabs wouldn't know about chili—they might even think the country in South America was involved. Their leaders would be called together in emergency meeting and they would decide that internal dissension had broken out in the United States, a new and bloody civil war, and they would conclude that this was the time for them to strike, to send their valiant troops across the seas and conquer America."

"Maybe I'd better call off this chili-cookin'," I said, always anxious to avoid a war.

"No," said Mrs. Bartholomew. "Keep stirring your chili. If those Arabs come over, we'll just turn B'nai B'rith loose on them."

We now noted the presence of a small plane which was buzzing Terlingua and on each buzz discharging hundreds of fluttering yellow cards. This aeronautical pamphleteering, I learned later, had its origin back in Dallas and could be traced to the sapient writings of Frank X. Tolbert. Mr. Tolbert made it clear in one of his columns that the Terlingua Confrontation was for men only, that no women would be allowed on the Dallas planes, and this meant wives. Old X. then demonstrated the depth of his wisdom by saying: "Girls can go, provided they are good-looking and got good builds."

Dallas women, being of the opinion that they are equal to men, began grumbling. Then word somehow got to them that some Swedish movie actresses were coming from Los Angeles. Their grumbling grew shrill, which is a physical impossibility. They organized. They formed the Terlingua Women's Auxiliary and Territorial Service and enlisted the aid of a pilot named Delmo Johnson. They had their yellow cards printed, sixteen thousand of them, and Delmo Johnson rained them down on the crowd at Terlingua. These cards were engraved with veiled threats of the type employed by Lysistrata and her girl friends during the Peloponnesian War. There were also some "foreign aid" packages dropped. They contained the Auxiliary's official flag—a pair of pink lace panties bearing the organization's initials. Some of the people there at Terlingua got quite a shock when they saw the flag with those initials. Also in the "foreign aid" packages were bandages made from pink nightgowns, small bottles of Alka-Seltzer, and clap medicine.

Anne Leary gathered some of the yellow cards for me; and Dick Rogers, the Alpine banker, told me later that many of them fell into Dirty Woman Creek, a circumstance fraught with symbolism. Among the messages were:

IT'S HOW YOU MAKE IT LONG.
CONGRATULATIONS! YOU GET THE CHILDREN.
RATON DE ESCUSADO (RAT RESIDUE).
A CHICK IN THE SACK IS BETTER THAN A CHIP
ON THE RANGE.
IF IT'S YOUR TURN, DON'T!
WE CAN GET IT FOR YOU WHOLESALE.
AT YOUR AGE, A LITTLE DAB'LL DO YA.

And there were some that were vulgar. Dallas had suffered a greater collapse of morals than I ever suspected. There was a report around that one Dallas wife had put cracker crumbs in her husband's sleeping bag.

And what of Ole X. Tolbert who was largely responsible for this revolt of the angels? He just plain deserted his champion, Fowler, in Fowler's hour of trial and agony. Tolbert couldn't stay put. For a while he was out with Ranch Manager Harold Wynne inspecting the *al fresco* toilets. He was particularly interested in a privy which he later described, in one of his cultural columns, as the deepest one-holer on earth. This particular privy stands over an abandoned mine shaft and Harold Wynne was quoted as saying: "When you open the door of that outhouse you can hear the voices of people singing in China."

Mr. Tolbert also turned his back on chili and sought out a man named Cobos from Alpine. This Cobos set a large pot over a mesquite fire, some distance from the Inn, and cooked up a mess of son-of-a-bitch stew, and then he barbecued some beef and laid out some bread and pickles and *salsa* and began charging people $2 a head for his fodder. Tolbert bought some. Then he moved on to a trailer belonging to a

179

couple of spoilsport interlopers from Abilene—men who had come equipped to cook their own chili and barbecue, and who did it. Tolbert ate some.

Back on the porch I continued stirring my chili and from time to time I tasted it. By this time Wick Fowler had enlisted an official taster in the person of a robed monk called Father Duffy. This Father Duffy wore a cowl and was barefooted and was a member of the hippie contingent flown in from Los Angeles. I never did find out who was responsible for the presence of those gorgeous birds.

This Father Duffy had taken a shine to me at the beginning and began hanging around my end of the porch, which made me nervous because I always suspect guys like him of being a little faggy, if there is such a thing as being a little faggy. He kept plucking at my sleeve and asking me questions in some kind of guru language, and finally I had to caution him gently, and let him know without offending him that he was getting in my way. I said: "Listen, you smelly son of a bitch, either take my confession and grant me absolution, or get your shabby ass offa this porch." For some reason he was nettled by my words and promptly transferred his allegiance to Fowler. He took up a position on the parched ground directly in front of Fowler and from then on, about once every six or eight minutes, Wick would extend a long spoon of his chili across the apron of the porch and Father Duffy would take a lick of it and cry out, "Soooooooper!"

There was another hippie wearing a Portuguese stocking cap, who spent his time meditating and never reaching any conclusions, but he didn't bother anybody; and a third who looked almost respectable except for the hair. This one spent a solid hour hovering around and heckling me about the rebel yell. He'd taunt me with, "Ole Yankee peckerhead, don't know from nothin' about the rebel yell! Dumber'n a ox. Dirty Ole Yankee." After this sort of abuse had gone on for a long time, I began sassing him back, telling him to go pick his cotton and go whup his slaves, else I'd sick a prairie dog on him. He didn't stop. When I interrupted my cooking to go to the Terlingua Public Library, he stood outside yelling about how I was dumb about the rebel yell.

Then there were the Swedish actresses. I couldn't swear to their number, but people said there were six of them. Occasionally I would catch glimpses of them, coming out of the Inn lobby, or going in, always accompanied by Texas-looking gentlemen who kept themselves busy copping feels. I had personal contact with only one Swedish actress, an interlude that was quite pleasant. She was heading for the booze department inside the Inn when she happened to notice me and, recognizing powerful *machismo* instantly, she veered off and came over to me. I was stirring my chili. As she came up to me, her eyes aglitter, she was saying in a soft voice: "Sock it to me sock it to me sock it to me sock it to me."

"Can't you see I'm cookin'?" I said.

She said: "Sock it to me sock it to me sock it to me sock it to me." She was doing it without any Swedish accent. She moved forward and rubbed against me frontways—*her* frontways. Then she rubbed against me backways. Hers. I thought, my god, this girl will do almost anything just to get a bowl of my chili.

But I am a pro, a dedicated man. I could have just thrown my tools to the floor and called out for Art Leibson or even Wick Fowler to take over my cooking, and hauled her off somewhere and socked it to her. I kept my cool, but only because of my age.

"Listen, kid," I said to her, "I'm a fella happens to favor Norwegians over Swedes."

"Marvelous!" she exclaimed. "My mother's Norwegian! Also my father!"

I bent to my work. I still think the Chili Appreciation

Society people sicked her on me, hoping that I'd respond affirmatively to her invitation and sock it to her, hoping that I'd foul out. She went away greatly hurt, deeply wounded, *hungry*. Illinois honor had triumphed again.

As soon as the girl had departed, I realized that the moment had come for a delicate procedure. It was time for me to put in the controversial beans. I must confess that I was jittery. I knew that I would be violating holy Texas tradition. But I grat my teeth and went ahead with it. I reached into my bag and brought forth two cans of pinto beans and a can opener. Ignoring the grizzled ranchers who were standing back of the rope, still studying my technique, I began opening the cans.

Nobody spoke. Nobody said a word.

I removed the lid from the pot and began dumping the beans into the chili.

It started with a small murmur. Then one of the old men said slowly and distinctly:

"He's done lost th' war."

"Shore has," said another. "Seemed like sucha nice fella, too."

And a third said: "Disgustin'. Makes yer ass pine fer a dippa snuff."

Defiantly I emptied both cans of beans into my pot and five minutes later I notified the knaves Tierney and Rives that I was ready for judgment. They checked with Wick Fowler and he said he was ready.

The two pots were carried across the porch, through the unruly crowd, and placed on a table beside the microphone. The judges were summoned from the salt flats out front. The two contestants, the three judges, and Rives and Tierney lined up before the table. Bandana blindfolds were tied round the heads of Hallie Stillwell, Floyd Schneider, and Mayor David Witts. The moment of truth was upon us.

A chili-feeder took a spoonful of Fowler chili and fed it

into Hallie Stillwell's mouth. She began to roll it around on her tongue and then suddenly she winced. She told me later that the Fowler chili made the little muscles in her heels, the Achilles tendons, begin snapping and popping, and she had the feeling that wisps of smoke were coming out of her shoes. The stuff was not fit for human consumption. She gasped a couple of times and said, "Let me try the other brand." She was given a spoonful of my chili. Beneath the bandana kerchief she was observed smiling with pleasure approaching ecstasy.

"This is it," she said. "This is the best. Easy."

"That," cried Bill Rives, a strong note of anger in his voice, "appears to be a vote for the Yankee."

A cheer went up from the crowd. The populace had, after observing me in action for several hours, and after watching the rude antics of the Dallas mob . . . the populace had slowly transferred its affection to me, although there was one blonde woman in the front ranks of the crowd, a woman with a behind suited to the needs of a brewery horse, who had not surrendered to my charm, and who now howled: "Go home, you crooked Yankee bastard!"

The next judge on the line was Floyd Schneider. They fed a spoonful of Fowler chili into his maw. He made as if he was tasting the finest food ever set before mortal man. He went "Mmmmmmmmmmmmm!" a dozen times and plastered a beatific, gargoyle grin on his coarse-featured puss. He spent a long time getting that Austin slop down his gullet and then—I'm sure this beer-sodden creature could *see* out from under his blindfold—he stuck his tongue out at my chili. Stuck a great big old bull-tongue out, like a snotty little boy. Then he hollered: "Ah castses mah un-by-assed vote faw mah fren' Ole Wick Fow-luh!" A man of questionable integrity.

The moment came now for the deciding vote. A hush fell over the crowd. Even the drunks were quiet. A mountain bobolink cackled in the sagebrush. A desert porcupine whickered back of the Opera House. A coyote spoke longingly to the burning sun. And someone rammed a spoonful of chili into the mouth of David Witts, lawyer, rancher, Mayor of Terlingua, traitor to all that is good and true in American life.

The newspaper accounts were in fearful disagreement about the succeeding few moments, but *I know* what happened. I was standing beside this shyster Witts. If I had been a muleycow my right hind hoof would have been in his coat pocket. I was that close to him.

Some said it was my chili that threw David Witts into seeming convulsions. I know better. What they put in his mouth was a concoction of fiery ancho chiles laced with shreds of bull leather—Wick Fowler's chili. That's what scorched the Witts gullet and took the enamel off the Witts teeth. He was, manifestly, miscast as a judge in a chili contest. A stick of peppermint would have stung his tongue and set his eyes to watering. The bite of overseasoned Fowler chili led him to snatch a handkerchief from his pocket and start swabbing the interior of his mouth. He huffed and puffed and writhed in agony. He outdid all Barrymores, gasping and gurgling, and when he thought the timing was right, he blurted out in agonized accents that his taste buds had been crippled, paralyzed, stunned. He didn't say *whose* chili had done this to him; he simply gasped out that the contest would have to be called a Mexican standoff, a draw, a tie, and that there would be a second Confrontation at a later date. In Sam Goldwyn's memorable words, the whole affair was a carriage of misjustice.

In a public event of this far-reaching significance it is always wise to have a clear-headed evaluation from an unprejudiced outside person. At the height of the cookery a Michigan tourist and his wife drove into the arena. The man

184

surveyed the scene and approached Tom Leary and said: "What in the name of time is goin' on here?"

"It's a contest," said Leary, "to see who is the greatest chili cook in the world." The Michigan man rolled this over in his mind. Then he said: "You people down here do this type of thing frequently?"

"Oh, sure," said Leary. The man from Michigan turned to his wife.

"Well," he observed rather sadly, "it's like I been telling you. The whole damn country's gone off its rocker."

When it was over the press crowded in and asked me for a final statement. I spoke with considerable tact and restraint, saying:

"Let us bind up our wounds. Wick Fowler is a sterile screwworm fastened to the hide of America's culinary elite. Back in New York when the time came to break up the Yankees, we broke them the hell up. The day has now come to wipe out this arrogant Chili Appreciation Society and to arrest Wick Fowler for subornation of chili. Only then will the future of good chili be secure in the great State of Texas."

TWENTY

Thus ended 1967's only month-long weekend.

The last I saw of the Dallas crowd they were heading west toward El Paso and Juarez to roll some drunks.

I returned quietly to Alpine, to pick up the threads of my previous life, to forget the tumult and the shouting of Terlingua. It is true that I have built a house on the side of a mountain in Alpine. This came about after my wife and I had explored half a dozen places for a future home—a home away from the East that has grown more hideous with each passing year, the East where a man can no longer live and move about in comfort and good health.

Forty years living in and around New York City was a god's plenty. We looked again in Hawaii. We drove around Florida. Shoulder-to-shoulder living, shoulder-to-shoulder housing, shoulder-to-shoulder eating . . . quite possibly shoulder-to-shoulder other things, in both places. No better than New York.

We read a magazine article singing the praises of Corpus Christi in Texas, and someone told us that Galveston was a wonderful place. We went to look at these Texas Gulf towns and we'd probably have chosen Corpus save for the fact that we couldn't find the kind of house we wanted, facing that beautiful water.

We heard of an interesting house for sale in Alpine and by this time we knew the town fairly well, and headed west. We looked at the house and liked it, but somehow the notion entered my head that I would like to build—something I'd never gone through. I asked our friend Harry Carpenter if there were any good building sites around Alpine.

"Right up this road," said Harry. We got in his car and ran about a quarter of a mile up the highway known as the Loop Road and then Harry Carpenter drove zigzag up a steep hill, to a wide shelf of land ninety feet above the highway level. As we made the ascent we had been talking and then I got out of the car and turned around and looked, and I pointed my index finger at my feet and said:

"Right by god here. This is where I'm gonna live."

Even though I met with frequent roadblocks, even though I resolved several times that I'd pick up my marbles and move on, even though Alpine's traditions held true and I encountered as many grasping and greedy people as I had met with in my years around Broadway and Hollywood—all I needed to do was to go climb up that mountain again and look west . . . and I stayed with it. I refused to let the sharpers drive me away.

Our glistening white Spanish-style house, with its handsome red tile roof, faces in the direction where Destiny dwells—to the west, out across Alpine to Marfa and Van Horn and eventually to the golden city of El Paso del Norte, now become our metropolis. My hill turns its back on the degenerate chawbacons of the Dallas–Austin–San Antonio axis. Consumers of mush picante. Eaters of fricassee of buffalo chip. Wolfers down of billygoat sweetbreads. Readers of Frank X. Tolbert.

The old wounds *will* heal, of course. Chili will be forgotten and chicken-fried gristle will once again prevail in Brewster County. Once more Pippa will pass. For better or for worse, in sickness and in health, till death or divorce do us part, I am today a Texan.

I have a New Jersey newspaper friend named Edward Norton who says of chili: "I'd rather eat the bindings off a set of Winston Churchill." He has written to me:

"Your decision is one more confirmation of my belief that you are a great and unique American writer. Other writers withdraw to Westport, Connecticut, to Bucks County, Pennsylvania, to Big Sur in California. But *you.* You retire to Alpine, Texas. Man, that's style!"